THE MAZE IN THE ENGLISH PARK

A Historical Crime Novella

Elizabeth von Witanovski

ISBN 978-1-955156-86-8 (paperback)
ISBN 978-1-955156-87-5 (hardcover)
ISBN 978-1-955156-88-2 (digital)

Rushmore Press LLC
1 800 460 9188
www.rushmorepress.com

Printed in the United States of America

To the three most important men in my life: my wonderful, brilliant sons, who are the reason behind this book, and my husband, Peter, whose extraordinary support made this book possible.

"The theatre is so endlessly fascinating because
it's so accidental. It's so much like life."

—Arthur Miller

CONTENTS

Karel looked at his friend and asked slowly, "Dead? Who's dead?"

Josef sat there, clutching the cup full of strong red wine. He pressed his mouth on the brim, more to control the tremble than to sip. He was shattered by the events of the last hours. He saw clearly the mythical Fates: one holding the spindle and another pulling the thin thread of his life, while the third one, Atropus, "the one who cannot be turned," moved her hand, with glistening shears, closer…

ACT ONE

1880s Prague, Austro-Hungarian Empire

aindrops hit the windowsill. Josef looked up. The dark night outside didn't allow him to see the rain gliding down the window panes. Not even a warm summer night like this one could permeate the yard-thick stone walls. Josef shivered as he took off his dinner jacket.

Until a few years back, he'd lived in Vienna. He was certain that everything good and exciting happened only in Vienna, with its vibrant social scene, concert halls, museums, balls, and opera. There was always something interesting to engage in and fascinating people to photograph or to be photographed with. But then events of larger proportion changed things for him forever. He'd been underage and unable to oppose his mother's decisions then.

It was as if the earthquake down on the French Riviera had turned the whole of 1887 inside out. That was in February of that year. Two thousand people had perished. Mother had been traveling in Italy. The horrifying event had made her rush back to the safety of their Viennese palace.

Then anarchists had ruined the entire ball season with their "idiotic demands," as she put it. The demonstration they'd organized ended in bloody beatings and imprisonments. In the following months, several shocking assassinations had been only "a logical reaction"; Josef privately sympathized with the idea of anarchism. His mother had been shocked.

Some of the assassins had been captured and executed. Regardless of the danger, Josef had tried to get connected, secretly and unsuccessfully, with an anarchist cell. His mother had uncovered some pamphlets he'd written, stuffed in his closet: "Idiot!" In the same week, portraits of anarchists—wanted, alive or dead—had been posted all over the city. Vienna was on alert.

Mother had dispatched a few letters to her Prague address in Bohemia, her late husband's ancestral home. Several days later, she'd received a telegram—all had been prepared as she'd instructed. Josef had been packed and sent to the Bohemian capital to keep him out of trouble.

Two marble giants holding the meandering balcony looked as dark and glossy as Josef remembered them from his childhood. His family's Prague palace had been closed for years, with only one servant, old Anton, living there. Several times a year, a few hired staff were brought in to keep the place in order. Josef remembered the place fondly from his childhood; he'd spent part of his visits there on Anton's shoulders, galloping through the vast park.

He made himself at home in the guest quarters overlooking the garden. Mother wasn't there to object. Small rooms but quieter. Josef's wealth allowed him to settle in comfortably and forget all about Vienna. He, however, could not find any comfortable way to fit into Prague's high society. He wished his father was still alive. Josef did not have any appetite for exploring the nightlife—or the day life—alone. The constant fights of the Czech and German students had nothing to do with him. He did not have an opinion on the matter and was not keen on forming one anytime soon. Anarchism did not seem to have arrived here yet. Mother got it right again.

He was bored. He allowed time to pass almost undetected, with days filled with private studies and some sports around the broad river. He started yearning for some exciting company.

Then one day, everything changed. Baron von Silber's calling card was on the polished silver tray. He'd arrived from Vienna for his annual pilgrimage. He took Josef under his wing without much asking. The National Theater had a new star in its ensemble. Baron von Silber introduced the two young men with his usual efficiency.

Raindrops hit the tall window. More rain! Josef was too tired now to go in the garden and run, bare-chested and unseen, in the warm summer night's shower.

"Some other time, then." He sighed. His stiff collar bounced, tossed on his bed. After a short struggle the heavy golden cufflinks gave in and he put them on the commode that served as his nightstand. This one had come centuries ago as part of a dowry— dramatically carved, heavy exotic wood was inlaid with colorful pieces of marble depicting the Judgment of Paris on its desktop. Josef's eyes ran the curve of Aphrodite's naked body. As the story went, it became a hiding place for the future bride's lover. It was like reading Boccaccio's Decameron. Josef felt embarrassed, but it never ceased to tickle his funny bone. Ancestors! He shook his head and fell backward onto the soft featherbed.

It was some dinner last night! Even now his palate could detect the heavy cream sauce with lingonberries. Baron von Silber never held back when he had the opportunity to show off.

The baron's "Prague Week" was the event to commemorate his poor late wife. Of an old Bohemian-German industrialist family, young, beautiful, and wealthy, she died in childbirth in Prague nineteen years ago.

Painfully, the anniversary of his wife's death was his only child's birthday. He'd decided to honor that bittersweet day every year—the first party in Prague; then, a week later, one more in Vienna. Both celebration dinners were always a grand lesson in opulence. "My late wife would have loved it this way…"

"Bad taste of the new money!" Josef's mother never failed to note afterward.

The glittering of the fine, ornately cut, brilliant Bohemian crystal competed with the shimmering of jewels. Silver and gold were on display wherever eyes could reach. Fresh flowers arranged into high, fragrant pyramids alternated with glistening silver trays full of cascading exotic fruits. Silver plates in the shape of giant shells were laid with rows of oysters placed on crushed ice. Slowly melting, it kept dripping into the orchids placed on the deep silver tray underneath in an inescapable staccato all evening. Course after course of unusual meals was laid in front of enthusiastic, fashionable guests in perfectly sumptuous choreography. Ruby-red Venetian blown-glass bowls with solid gold handles held water with cut lemons to help the gourmands' fingertips stay clean. Delicious petit fours and bonbons seduced guests throughout the drawing rooms of this vast, modern apartment. It was furnished à la mode, as pompous as its owner was dressed. Looking at his lively company, the loud, vivacious mix of German and French around the long mahogany table covered in heavy damask brocade, the color of the large emerald pinned into his cravat, the baron knew that he had triumphed again.

The baron's only daughter, Sophie-Ann von Silber, sat across the table from Josef. In the subtle light of myriad candles, the glistening of diamond stars in her hair gave her a fantastic sparkling halo. The effect was stunning. The effect on Josef was absolute. Sophie-Ann looked breathtaking that night.

No one could have guessed how spoiled and capricious she could be. Josef knew that too well. They'd become friends as children in Vienna. Their fantastic games were the highlight of his solitary, boring childhood. When she started turning into a spoiled young woman, he observed with sadness the sudden minefield she'd laid between the two of them.

"I have been bred for princes," she would whisper into his face before kissing him at the bottom of the green marble staircase at their palace in Vienna.

Josef woke up from his day-dreaming. He looked toward the dark windows and listened for more rain. Then he reached into his pocket. The letter he pulled out felt like hot cinders in his hand. Ever since it arrived in the middle of dinner last night, Josef had been eager to read it. But now he put it carefully next to him. He watched it like something venomous while he kept undressing. Raindrops hit the windowsill again, much stronger this time. Josef was glad he'd left all the windows closed last night. Now he could stay in bed and read that "Damn reply from Karel!" he said angrily out loud. He pushed himself up against the new high wooden headboard framed by detailed carvings of berries and ginkgo leaves. His pillow tucked comfortably under his head, he reached for the letter.

When it had been delivered to him at the dinner table last night, he'd been confused. He'd opened it carefully on his lap and glanced down. He'd found it almost impossible to conceal his anger. Karel had written it on Josef's own writing paper! Josef immediately had pushed the letter deeply into his pocket. He did not notice Sophie-Ann's sharp, jealous glance from across the table.

For the length of the evening, he'd successfully pretended that the letter never existed. He'd engaged in the amusing conversation about the hidden skills of the men present.

"I think I could make a good spy," he'd mused.

"No, you could not. You have too much of the old aristocratic honor," someone had replied, and they'd all laughed.

The latest of Baron von Silber's brilliant social moves for which he was known was Karel Bernini and Josef, Count von Kaplitz's surprising misalliance, which he'd skillfully arranged. This one was the most welcome, amusing relief for social gossipers in the midst of the unpleasant battle over the demolition project of the Old Prague Jewish ghetto.

Karel was the youngest of the well-established, popular theater dynasty of actors, himself the rising star of the Prague National Theater. Josef was heir to his father's important name, the indisputable future star of the Viennese political scene, equally ambitious, and just a few months younger than the thespian.

The baron had known Josef since the day he and his late wife had been invited to Josef's christening. He'd observed with disillusion Josef's father's turn against the mainstream politics of the Viennese court. His sudden early death had solved many political headaches. Baron von Silber himself had navigated that scene with ease and without scruples since his own youth. He was not excited about the new proposed social reforms. The honor of old aristocrats remained foreign to him. It was rumored that he had cooperated with the secret police on several occasions.

To the young, inexperienced Josef, it seemed implausible. The jovial baron? Nonsense!

The baron saw in Josef his own young self, the way he'd hoped he would have looked at his own son. Josef looked like his elegant French mother. The slant of his eyes came from her long, aristocratic bloodline from Gascony. The baron noticed that Josef carried a knife in his pocket. It was the same kind the baron carried himself—the locking thin-bladed gem of Spanish origin. The baron had heard from someone in Vienna that Josef had a vast collection of small cold weapons. Perhaps he was not as angelic as he always presented himself to be. The baron liked him even more for that.

Karel's mother, the incomparable Adele Bernini, had her dressing room in the National full of fresh bouquets every evening when the baron resided in Prague. Now and then, one of them included a calling card. He had been impatiently waiting for her answer for years.

Karel looked more like his Italian father. Stocky, dark-skinned, with a straight spine, he was sure of himself. His mane of dark blond hair came from his mother. He was jealous and appalled by the baron's free mores. He felt the superiority of his family over the baron's family of social-climbers. He kept that carefully to himself.

Karel and Josef became immediately close. Josef decided, purely based on his instincts, to reveal his fascination with anarchism to Karel. He'd read in the Wiener Blatt paper about the leader of the anarchists, an elusive, dangerous man, whose mark was a black jingle bell with a capital A inside. The police had no information about the man's whereabouts. "He could be anywhere!" Josef said to Karel. There was the same portion of fear and excitement in it.

Josef was annoyed that Karel did not want to talk about any of that at all. Karel never even introduced him to his other friends who hung around backstage now and then, those beyond theater circles. There was always something else, something "we must do." Josef was convinced, more and more, that there were some anarchists among them. They had to be!

The baron had his opinions definitely formed, and he chuckled after hearing Josef's new theory. "Anarchists? U Pinkasu? My young friend, it is all one big, well-planned advertisement. That pub is the most perfect post-performance watering hole! That's all. Besides, actors are not interested in politics, only in themselves!"

Josef looked at him, surprised. He was convinced otherwise and almost said it. There was, however, a sudden uncomfortable feeling, some false note in the baron's voice that made Josef keep his latest observation to himself;

Not long ago, he'd entered Karel's dressing room unexpectedly.

Karel was just finishing some writing. He'd swept it swiftly down onto his lap. "My directorial notes," he'd explained. When he tried to move it into his pocket later during their conversation, Josef had been certain that he'd seen the anarchistic mark—the black icon of a capital letter A in a full circle.

Since that moment, Josef kept waiting for his chance to ask Karel about it.

The opportunity arose during one of their numerous walks.

They were about to pass the A sign painted hastily on a garden wall. Karel stopped and started looking for something on the ground. He picked up a small fragment of dark-brown roof tile. Then he stepped toward the white wall and, in front of a surprised Josef, encircled the capital letter A. Josef was standing behind him with an unpleasant feeling that someone was observing them, but then, his friend kept drawing underneath it! Karel drew a jingle bell. Josef glanced around in fear. Karel added the capital A to that circular shape.

"But this is…" Josef was scared but intrigued. Karel grabbed his hand, and they started running into the labyrinth of Old Prague's narrow medieval streets.

"That's the mark…" Josef shouted in between large strides as they ran up the steep cobblestone-paved paths toward the castle. "Of the … unknown … the archenemy…"

Karel stopped. They were safely far enough now. This street was a shortcut, always dark and empty. Josef stood opposite Karel. Both young men's heads were down on their chests, panting, trying to catch their breaths.

Josef tried to finish his thoughts in between each gulp of air. "You should not … be drawing that mark. … Nobody knows who that guy is … He writes the most vicious pamphlets … He organizes … He's very powerful … It is all very…" He searched for a good word. Dangerous did not seem to quite suffice.

In the next moment, in front of Josef's shocked eyes, Karel dropped his pants down to his knees.

Underneath was his olive-skinned naked body. Generous dark curly hair filled up and spilled out from his groin. Josef held his breath, unable to scream, unable to react. They were far from everything; nobody would hear Josef's scream. Why? His worst nightmare was materializing here, with the face of his closest friend.

"Please, don't do that," whispered Josef. His hand fingered the blade in his pocket.

Karel looked at him, apparently confused "What?"

Josef woke up from his nightmare. His fingers moved away from the knife.

Karel was pointing, next to his penis, of a peculiar shade of brown. "There…"

Josef's eyes, coming out of shock, were finally willing to focus where Karel kept pointing—at the small tattoo in the curls next to his sex.

It was the black jester's jingle bell holding the capital letter A within its circle.

Josef sat down heavily on the cobblestones. Karel pulled up his pants and sat down next to him. After a moment, in which Josef did not try to form any words, Karel said, "So you know it now."

Silence.

"I am in your hands."

Then, almost apologetically, Karel added, "I only write…" And since there was no answer in sight, he said, "It really stinks here."

They gave sidelong glances at each other and burst into loud, relieved laughter.

"Come on, you!" Karel pulled Josef up from the ground. Holding each other around their shoulders, they started walking in unison in long steps, as only young boys can.

When they arrived in front of the stage door, Karel became serious again. "This is all much too dangerous. Don't ask me anything else. What you see when we are together stays there. It is a question of life or death—and not just yours or mine."

Josef's youth rushed forward. "I can help. I have connections in Vienna already."

Karel looked back at his friend. "This is anarchism we are talking about." Then, he added in a voice an octave lower, where he would put it for his Othello, "If you are serious, you would have to prove it." With the authority of the older one, he added further, annoying Josef, "But still, you are too young for such things!"

Raindrops seemed to hit the windowsill much harder now.

Josef briefly ran his eyes over the letter. It was Karel's passionate political attack of Josef's "pseudo-diplomatic excuses." Then he glanced down at Karel's signature. "God! He is insane!"

His friend had signed with his full name, to which he'd added his anarchistic mark.

Josef sat up. This was typical Karel, late at night. He was always flying high after his brilliant performances, ending without exception in deafening ovations. The star! He needed to be in the leading role under any circumstances. He made the entire empire think that he was the elusive leader. The complete police force was after him!

The truth was, Josef von Kaplitz deeply admired Karel Bernini. He always immediately forgave him for everything, even now, no matter how annoyed. He felt that if anyone had the right to be aloof, it was this genius friend of his—

Josef did not finish his thought when he heard the raindrops again.

Now he realized that he had been mistaken. It wasn't the rain; it was sand from the path in his garden. "Karel! At last!" Josef knew his friend would come to apologize after all.

Barefoot and half-dressed, he started down the old sandstone staircase with a smile. While slipping from one softly worn-down step to another, his left hand tried to tuck the stiff letter into his pocket. His right hand was gliding on the wooden handrail, its silky texture heating up by his quick movement. His palm's memory could evoke this pleasure anywhere, anytime. The overwhelming feeling of sudden uncomplicated happiness caused him to close his eyes.

Josef was quickly down at the back gate. He jumped down customarily from the third step. As always, he landed on both feet simultaneously, just like he would finish his favorite dance, the mazurka, in a ballroom. He kept smiling.

The long, enormous key turned the blackened ironwork of the heavy lock. The door swayed in. Josef stayed behind it for a second as he planned to surprise Karel and make him laugh. He suddenly hopped in front of his friend in the submissive pose of a jester.

"What are you doing?" Sophie-Ann was disgusted. Her voice was cranky, full of tears and anger. "What took you so long? I am cold. I've been shivering here for an hour!"

Josef could not believe his eyes. She immediately pushed around him and in the door. He tried to stop her. "Come back! What do you think ...?"

Her smile was drunken and cute. This was one of the moments when she looked like a sweet little girl, to be protected and taken care of. She just stood there, petite, looking smaller than usual.

"How did you get here in this hour?" he asked and then shook his head. "Why, of course!" Josef remembered now. "Your birthday present. The new Benz, right?"

She widened her smile. "The Number Three," she said and lifted one eyebrow. She was no more a little girl. "Bertha Benz took it sixty-six kilometers! It's not even ten to get here from the King's Vineyards."

Josef glanced at her sideways. So this was another caprice of hers. "How could I forget?" Josef exhaled, suddenly very tired, and then said out loud, "Listen to me now. You will go home, and I'm off to bed."

Her voice changed again to that of a little girl's. "That's not polite to push me out like this! And I am thirsty..."

Josef gave in, as always, too soon. He hated himself for that. "All right, come, then. I will pour you some water. Nobody's here to wait on us, though," he warned. They started walking up the softly shaped sandstone steps. She dragged her drunken existence wearily behind him "Do you know that she was photographed with the new handheld camera?"

"Who?"

" Berta Benz, of course! The newest invention of modern photography! Papa will buy me one next month in New York."

"My father already has one," Josef said this only to annoy her. Now he was caught in his own pain. After a few steps, overcoming tears, he corrected himself. "Had one."

Sophie-Ann couldn't have cared less. "You were not amusing last night." She smoothly took on an annoyed, argumentative tone.

At this moment, Josef was not ready to practice any diplomacy. "I think you were full of yourself. You did not pay any attention. The minister and your father were both very compl—"

Her envy couldn't allow him to finish. "Compliments from my father? Blah blah blah!" With her voice an octave higher because of her anger and jealousy, she started mimicking her father. "Oh, look how elegant Josef looks tonight! Did you hear how engaging Josef's speech was? Josef is the most brilliant young man in Vienna! The future prime minister!" She stopped, breathless from her speech, and stamped her foot. "I am sick of it! I am sick of being his daughter! I am sick of his rapturous speeches about you! I hate him! He wants you! That's all he really wants—for you to be his!"

Josef pulled her out of the stairwell and into the first drawing-room. Although nobody was around, he could not listen to her accusations without feeling ashamed of her. She looked at him, surprised, and wiggled her arm from his hand. "Ouch! It hurts!" Her dark eyebrows met above her not-too-delicate nose. "I am thirsty." Now she whined like a five-year-old again. Josef walked into the dark and lit the oil lamps.

"Be there light!" said Sophie-Ann with the irony and declamation of a heroine from a Greek tragedy. She was still dressed in her lavish golden Worth of Paris evening gown. It was not the gown her mother would have chosen for her. The diamond-and-pearl stomacher accentuated her tiny waist. Her full breasts were supporting a diamond-and-spinel necklace. Like the diamond stars in her hair, they too reflected the colors of the spectrum on the ceiling and walls, once the warm light hit their facets. Josef noticed how lovely she still looked even now, in this tired hour between midnight and dawn.

He wanted to kiss her. He wanted it very much. He had to do it. He turned.

"Have a seat." He pointed to the fragile gilded chair and quickly walked out.

Sophie-Ann looked around. She could not believe how backward this palace remained. She spotted some art nouveau objets d'art but looked away, unimpressed. It was nothing she hadn't seen or possessed already. She stopped in front of the looking glass and stared at her reflection admiring her perfect complexion, her numerous diamonds, and the curve of her chin. Her mind, however, was preoccupied with her newest diversion. She came here for an answer. Her eyebrows moved slightly out of place; her lips squeezed the corner of her mouth, distorting her lovely image. She would get what she wanted. She always did. Sophie-Ann turned and crossed quickly to the door.

Josef was bringing her fresh water. She would wait for him.

He pushed the door open with his back, both hands holding the heavy tray. Sophie-Ann quickly pulled out the letter from his pocket, where she'd spotted it when she arrived, and ran to the opposite corner. She was proud of herself. It was easier than she'd anticipated. She could not stop smiling. She had it!

She'd noticed the letter last night, the moment it was delivered to Josef during dinner. Her jealousy had flared up painfully as if some of her fine skin was caught in the lacing of her corset. It burned and hurt, and it made her nauseated. She had to find out who sent the letter!

And now, here it was. No doubt a billet-doux. She saw Josef's perplexed expression. That confirmed her suspicion. She was right— it was a love letter.

During the dinner, she could not think of anything else. She'd heard rumors of Josef's planned engagement to that wimp, old maid Mitrowitz girl. The old aristocracy? So what if Sophie's grandfather had bought his title? Who cared?

She was rich. She would be no less than a duchess one day. Now her bright mind was busy with dangerous deductions. The rumors were all about an arranged union. Well then, the love letter could hardly be from the Mitrowitz hussy. Then who was so impatient that the letter could not wait? Who would write in such a hurry, with such urgency that did not respect Josef's private affairs? That motif she understood exactly—a jealous lover. That was it. Josef had a secret lover! A lover who'd just found out about his engagement.

Sophie-Ann glanced at Josef across the room with the deep hate of a betrayed woman. Her lightly shaking hand flipped the letter open. She felt the venomous, distorted thrill of all the possibilities this letter held—the gossip in Prague, the gossip in Vienna, the scandal she could create, the scandal she would create.

"Give it back." Josef's calm voice interrupted the stream of her drunken, frantic schemes. He set down the tray, careful with the glasses and the jug of water. His arm stretched toward her. His palm was opened in the commonly recognized gesture. "Aninka?" Josef called her softly by the diminutive name from the time of their childhood games.

She hesitated. Her face started getting softer, an almost tender expression. Her bejeweled body swayed from side to side, as if she intended to start dancing. The diamonds glittered. Sophie-Ann's eyes were fixed on Josef.

Josef's palm started moving slowly toward her.

The clock on the mantel chimed three. Sophie-Ann woke up from her haze. She could not let him have his letter back. Not without at least glancing at it! Unable to read it clearly, she turned toward the closest lamp.

The light sharpened the letterhead and the writing. Her drunken mind sobered. Josef stopped. Sophie-Ann flipped the letter back and forth. Her eyes were moving from the letter to Josef and back.

What she was holding was no love letter.

She was staring at the famous mark of the unknown leader of the anarchists. All of the police of the Austro-Hungarian Empire were after this man. Nobody knew who he was. Now, Sophie-Ann, the only daughter of the high imperial minister, was looking at his name. She still could not comprehend.

A few days ago, she'd seen him as Hamlet, and he'd made her cry. She'd seen him in Cid—dark, handsome. She yearned to watch him over and over; she dreamed about his touch.

Her eyes kept looking at the black circle and the jingle bell. Both of them had a capital A in their centers. She knew too well from her father what that mark meant—danger. That mark stood for murders, bombings, killers, and assassins! She stood there, glued to the spot, feeling faint. In disbelief, she turned the paper, hoping that this was just a mistake, just a sick joke. But the letterhead was Josef's golden coat of arms; she recognized his handwriting. Her horror turned to panic. Her mouth slowly opened, but she could not make a sound.

Her scream came unexpectedly so strong that Josef, who had started slowly moving toward her, stepped back. Then he charged forward.

Sophie ran to the windows, screaming for help. Josef was right behind her, almost touching the letter. She suddenly changed direction and was out the door.

Josef flew out and started after her down the stairs. He reached for the letter. As he pulled the paper out of Sophie's hand, his body was tossed backward. He landed painfully on the stone steps, holding the letter above his head. Sophie's body was tossed forward, and there was nothing to stop her.

Blood ran from underneath her hair as she lay head down on the stairs. Josef limped down to her and yelled out for help before realizing he was alone in the palace. He turned toward the injured girl.

"Wait, Sophie, wait. Everything is fine. Aninka, all is well. I'll be right back!"

Then, barely walking, with a sharp pain in his back and hip, he limped upstairs for water. He must get some towels to help Sophie clean up the wound and to bandage her head. She will kill me when she sees herself in the mirror, he thought, reminding himself of all the injuries that the two of them had gone through together during their childhood and her unfailing hysterics when she saw bruises on her pristine skin.

Exhausted from walking across the Charles Bridge, Josef was unable to make one more move. Only now, his injured back started to hurt. He stood in front of Karel's townhouse behind the National. Josef leaned toward the uneven wall of the one-story building, waiting, trembling. Once his strength returned, he lifted the door knocker and dropped it several times on the dark wooden gate. His exhausted arm dropped by his side, as if he'd just lifted the whole gate. After a couple more attempts, the noise woke Karel, and he came down. The small side door opened into the passage and hit the wall. Josef stumbled inside.

"Are you loaded?" Karel was sleepy, slightly irritated but amused at the same time. "Come on in. I will make us some coffee." And he was already stepping inside the house.

Josef did not move. His pale face reminded Karel of some modern paintings he and Adele had seen in an exhibition in Paris last summer. Josef finally spoke, but his words were inaudible. Karel moved his head closer and tried to listen more carefully. Then he suddenly processed Josef's words and grabbed his shoulders. He moved Josef easily as if he were a rag doll. He pulled him into the kitchen and sat him down on the bench by the tile stove. Still holding him firmly, as Josef looked like he was going to faint, Karel asked straight to his face, while pouring strong red wine into a cup, "Dead? Who is dead?"

Two young men stood over Sophie-Ann's quiet body. Josef felt weak and sat down above her on the cold sandstone steps. His sobbing filled up the vast space of the staircase all the way to the ceiling. The unforgiving Greek gods in the dramatic fresco didn't seem to sympathize with him. Josef cried inconsolably and with deep sorrow. Karel waited a moment and then put his hands on his friend's shoulders and firmly squeezed. "Josef, please … this is not your fault."

Josef briskly turned, tears still dripping from his cheeks. He snapped at Karel angrily. "It's all your fault! That stupid letter of yours! On my own writing paper! What were you trying to accomplish?"

Karel's hot blood moved his arms away from Josef's shoulders as if he'd been burned, and he attacked. "My fault? That's rich! Wasn't it you who promised, already weeks ago, to talk to your friends in Vienna and—"

"That was unreasonable. Diplomacy needs time. I needed only a few more days to—"

"Diplomacy is just another word for lack of courage!" Karel slapped his palm painfully on his thigh in anger and made a few random steps up the staircase.

Josef bent forward, his arched back expressing his misery. He stayed that way—quiet, resigned.

Karel sat down on the highest steps. Anger still was alive in every muscle of his young, expressive face; he stared into space. The night outside, turned into a deep blue, was getting lighter every minute. He heard the first birdsong. Out of habit, he started running his lines. Shakespeare. His Shakespeare. Rehearsals will start next week. He felt a familiar rush of excitement. His Romeo in the new production would be like nothing he'd ever done. His Romeo would be …

His mind grabbed the future tense and brutally bludgeoned it into the past.

The curtain fell heavily down and crushed him. Karel Bernini, the actor, existed no more. His brain finally sobered up; he looked at himself in hindsight in disbelief. Why had he written to Josef last night? Why had he signed it? It was too late for questions. He'd failed himself; he'd failed Josef, his friends. Mother. What would she say when she found out? He must go and see her immediately. No! That would endanger her now. What would she do? What would he do? Karel felt such pressure in his head that he feared he might go mad. He tried to just stare for now—to stare and feel nothing. He hoped that maybe, somehow, he would wake up, and all this would prove to be just one of his nightmares.

But it wasn't. In the end, his brain woke up and started working on full gear, as it always did in a crisis. His theater-trained mind took this catastrophic situation and turned it into a new role for him—the knight savior.

In a voice firmly placed as if the curtain was about to part on a new act, Karel said, "Josef, it's almost light. There's Sophie's car. We must push it in here before we leave. Now!"

Josef wiped his face and looked at Karel. He too was composed again. "I have to call the police first." He tried to stand up, disregarding his pain.

Karel shook his head and handed him the fatal letter. "You cannot do that."

"I have to. It is the honorable thing to—"

"You cannot. See?"

Josef looked at the letter, for the first time since the accident that night. He could not believe what he was looking at now.

True, he had plucked the letter from Sophie-Ann's hand, but at the same moment he'd lost the most significant piece of that paper— the letterhead. His coat of arms was printed in gold on one side, and on its reverse was Karel's full signature, together with his anarchist mark—the mark of the wanted, elusive archenemy of the Austro-Hungarian Empire.

That part was now tightly clenched in Sophie-Ann's hand.

If these were not their lives that were in stake, they could have appreciated the metaphor.

The Journey

The smell of coal filled up the platforms of Franz-Josef Station in Prague. Two young men walked up to the train. Their gait was a lesson in self-control. They both were good at that. They hesitantly passed by the first-class wagon, leaving it behind with longing glances. They found the second-class and sat down. A hissing noise came in blasts from different directions. The steam was let out of the engine in three mighty streams. Suddenly, very slowly, with the noise of chugging coming out of the chimney, the pistons started heavily moving the long lines of wheels forward. It was a beat of four, with a slow first. Puff—two-three-four, puff—two-three-four.

Josef tried to distract his mind, but he could hardly conceal his growing nervousness. Puff—two-three-four, puff—two-three-four. The steam engine carefully moved on the narrow tracks out of town and under the overhanging rocks by the river, meandering out to the Bohemian countryside and farther north. Josef wished they could have taken a different way out of Prague, but this was the first morning-train they could get to cross to Germany. The train started picking up speed and getting into the steady rhythm of equal four.

Karel was squeezed in the corner of the hard, thinly upholstered bench by the window. With his hat pulled over his face, he was pretending to be asleep. He could not face any conversation with

Josef now. He needed time to think. Could he stay somewhere in the Austro-Hungarian Empire and survive with friends' help? How could he accept pittance after living a privileged life? Would he have to go to the high mountains? Would he vanish much easier in an overpopulated metropolis? Berlin? Questions were swelling his brain. It was torture to think that his theater career was finished. It can't be over. I'm a born actor.

He was to become the actor of his generation. His exceptional talents had been recognized early on. His parents and grandparents— all actors—dotted on the talented boy. He had to find a solution! How could he live without theater? No, he could not.

The train started slowing down.

Josef's heart stopped. Police! They already know. He froze. He felt nauseated. They were going to murder him now. He had heard about people who "accidentally" fell from a running train. He stood up quickly, trying to figure out where to move.

A bright child's voice said loudly, "Look! We are on a bridge!"

Josef collapsed back into his seat. "A bridge."

Karel looked out the window and stood up. A bridge! A bridge high above the dark blue river. Maybe this was a sign. Jump, Karel, jump! It would be sure death down there on the huge boulders in the shallow river. When they found him, would they recognize him? The Great Bernini! Karel Bernini, the brightest young star of the National Theater in the Bohemian kingdom—dead! His eulogy would be on the first page of all the newspapers in the monarchy. The entire empire—no, all of Europe would hear about him. They surely would recognize him. Postcards with his photo portraits had been circulated everywhere for the last few years. At this very moment, his bust was being cast in bronze to assume a position of honor in the vestibule of the golden chapel of all Czechs—the National Theater. They surely would recognize him. Men would take off their hats, and women would make the sign of the crucifix with their hands. Some would break down in tears; some would kneel down … Here lies the Great Bernini…

With a loud new series of puffs, the steam engine picked up speed.

The bridge vanished into history. Karel sat down heavily and pulled his hat back over his face. Tears that had welled on the edges of his eyelids started running down his cheeks. Only now he remembered his mother again. Adele!

He would never be Hamlet to her Gertrude. He would never hold her in his arms. Karel bent forward, crushing his hat in his fists, and buried his face between knees.

By the time they arrived in Hamburg, Karel knew where they must go—to America.

"To America?" Josef turned his pale face toward Karel. They were standing in front of the station in Hamburg. Karel nodded and opened his mouth to explain, but Josef, putting stress on every word, as if talking to someone half-deaf, continued. "No. To London. The safest place in the world."

This was what Father would say. Josef had a clear concern, "I cannot leave and make them think that I am a murderer." His voice rose as he spoke more quickly. "I did not kill her! You know that. The honor of my family is at stake!"

"Shut up with your honor! It's our lives that are at stake, you idiot!"

Josef's numbness vanished. He turned toward Karel. With coldness and disgust that took Karel by surprise, Josef said, "You! You are just a servant. How can you understand?" Karel was astonished, but Josef did not notice. "I have obligations to my name, to my family, to our place in history. You know nothing about such things. Nothing at all! You are just a player. You in the role of the Archenemy is a vaudeville! You can go to the devil if you wish. I am going to London now, and then—soon, I hope—back to Vienna. I will make things right."

"You are mad!" Karel tried to grab Josef's arm and pull him toward the port. "We have to vanish. Can't you see? We are doomed! If we stay, we are dead!"

The melodramatic tone made Josef sick. This was Karel—"the star"—like too many times before, repeating some lines of one of his characters. He used to admire it. Now he felt appalled. Nothing was sacred to this pseudo-friend of his. Actors! Servants! Everything was just a play for them.

"Jesters with jingle-bells," hissed Josef, and he knew immediately that he would never be able to take back those words, that this was the end of the two of them.

He was not looking for any reconciliation. Not anymore. Karel reached for Josef's hand in a last attempt. "Josef, please…" Before he thought of words strong enough to change Josef's mind, a high-pitched female voice screamed for help.

The dynamic of the street changed in a second. People started running in all directions. Josef charged toward the voice without thinking. Then he stopped as quickly as he'd started running. When he turned back, Karel was gone. The street cleared out, a policeman arrived, and the poor crying woman explained what had happened to her.

Josef turned and started walking slowly toward the port. How long would his money last? Should he try to contact his mother? She never questioned his decisions. Would she this time? A newsboy with a large canvas bag full of newspapers hanging across his chest came running. As he was about to pass, Josef stopped him and bought one issue.

Josef's bewildered eyes were reflected on the front page. Accompanied by a photograph of Sophie-Ann taken in a ballroom, the headline read:

"Murder of Minister's Only Daughter in Prague!"

Josef dashed toward the port. Breathless, he inquired about the boat to London. "Hastings, in an hour," said the man behind the small glass window. Josef passed him a banknote and took the ticket.

His hand started to shake; his palm turned sweaty. He would not have made a good spy. This was the second time in two days that he felt paralyzed by fear. He was ashamed.

More than half an hour later, after sitting in a smoky pub, unable to move, unwilling to drink the schnapps he ordered, he walked out to the port to look for his boat. "Hastings?" he kept asking. Nobody knew. It was seven minutes to four, when, running up and down the docks in panic without getting any answer, too far from the ticket window, he finally stopped a sailor.

The man replied to Josef's German question in his native French. "Hastings isn't a boat." Then, after a second, while enjoying Josef's perplexed face, he added, "It's the port town she goes to. Follow me. I am on that one today, and I'm late." He tossed Josef's bag in haste over his shoulder and both men started to jog.

When Karel heard the female voice calling for help, that was a signal for him. He didn't wait but started running toward the port of Hamburg.

He ran for several blocks and then got lost in narrow streets. They reminded him of Prague's Old Town. His instincts warned him—these streets were not Prague. These streets saw more murders than any other town in Europe. Karel reached into his pocket, moved the switchblade knife into his hand, and hid it in his sleeve. He'd learned a knife fight for his theatrical performance. It already served him well once in Munich. His senses were all on alert as he jogged through the narrow alleys, jumping over puddles of unknown origin. The stench bothered his nose. He started to run again. He made the first possible turn and bumped into a young woman. Almost a child, she was making her living under the streetlight.

"How far to the docks from here?" he shouted at her.

She took her time in answering and slowly moved close to him. She had quick hands, but his were quicker. Karel locked her fragile body, dressed in rags, in his forearm. His knife pointed toward her painted face. She only gasped and tried to back up, but his fingers painfully squeezed her flesh. She opened her palm and spat at him in anger. He caught his pocket watch in midair, shoved her away, and ran.

Once out of the street maze, he touched the secret pocket with money and his papers. They would have to kill him to get to these. On a busy high street, a serious-looking older gentleman pointed Karel to the other side of Hamburg docks. That's where the boats for America were anchored.

Karel arrived at the port. From a distance, he already could hear the noises of the large crowd—a strong cacophony of shouts; laughter on the verge of hysterics; children's cries; loud conversations, trying to surpass the sounds of metal chains. High above it all were the mechanical movements of cranes loading the cargo into the bellies of ships.

Karel looked at the crowd of Germans waiting to board the vessel. He hesitated. The sea of bowler hats, hats with bows and flowers, hats with dead birds and veils, cheap blue straw hats of the nurses—they all kept moving slowly towards the large tall ship.

Questions about his future started bothering him again. What would he do in America? He was an actor; there was nothing else he could do. But, he argued with himself, I'm also young, athletic, and healthy. Maybe I'll be able to find a vaudeville theater somewhere there. The word held a bitter reminder of his quarrel with Josef. No, Karel would not waste more time thinking about his so-called friend. Back to his new plans. He realized that it was quite some time that he looked at the map of America—New York, Philadelphia, Boston ... Karel was not aware of any other places in America. He stopped. Then maybe, after all, London was a better idea. Unstoppable shivers started trembling throughout his lean body. Karel was exhausted and hungry. He pulled his coat closer and held himself in a tight embrace. His teeth would have rattled, had he not controlled it. Karel, the actor, closed his eyes and took several deep breaths. It never failed when he was stage-fright stricken. Nobody ever knew. Here, it helped again.

Karel slowly turned, still uncertain what to do next. His vivid imagination started creating landscapes with rivers, lakes, and rocks from the spills and small bits of garbage under his feet. He was traveling that new world, fully submerged in his colorful make-believe, where he was able to breathe freely. A long chain of monotone shouts somewhere behind him interrupted Karel's relaxing fantasy. He turned and gestured to the newsboy, whose voice came closer. A small coin between his fingers, he asked for one issue. The young man, a child really, quickly crossed to Karel, handing him the newspaper.

Karel stared at the front page. Most of the space was taken by a large photograph of a pretty young woman wearing a highly fashionable ball gown, with diamond stars in her hair. "Minister's Only Daughter Murdered in Prague! Anarchists Suspected!" shouted the German headline.

Karel walked up to the man standing nearby. "Where do I buy a first-class ticket to America?"

Obviously a burgher, the man measured Karel from the tips of Karel's now-dirty shoes up to his fine bowler. "That I can surely tell you. Where you might be able to get the second-class, that I wouldn't have been able to do."

Josef stood on the main street in Hastings. The air smelled of seawater, fish, piss, and beer. His legs were still weak from the boat. More than half an hour had passed since he stepped on the English shore, and the ground under him finally had stopped moving. He was a "dry-soil rat" after all. He was glad not to go to America. It was late in the day; the lamp-man had started lighting the gas street lamps with his long bamboo pole. His three-legged black-and-white dog was glued to his side. The gas lamps reacted at once to his light touch. He looked like a wizard creating lines of glowing dandelions.

Josef stopped watching. He knew he needed to change his clothes. The cut of his suit stood out in the mostly British crowd on the boat. His fear of being watched returned.

Locals pointed him to the tailor. As he was walking across the street, he noticed someone crossing at the same time. His heart started pounding. The nervous heat-wave drenched him in sweat. Josef entered the tailor's but then turned and immediately stepped back into the street. The suspicious man was looking at the window of a store that sold clocks. He did not seem to care about Josef, nor did he even acknowledge Josef's existence.

Josef tried to reason with himself. I must calm down. This is all nonsense. They do not know where I went. Nobody knows. He took several deep breaths and then reentered the tailor's shop.

A suit someone did not pick up was slightly bigger than Josef's size, but he liked it. The tailor said he would make alterations for Josef. "It will be ready in two hours."

He paid half of the amount immediately and stayed in the shop, citing a hurt ankle.

In just an hour he left the store, wearing his new gray afternoon suit. He forgot to limp. The well-fitted trousers, the elegant jacket over a nice white shirt, and a well-fitted vest turned his gait back into the walk of the well-bred self-confident gentleman he was.

He found the clean-looking inn recommended to him by the tailor and booked a room for the night.

The next day at noon, Josef walked out of the station in the British metropolis.

The year was 1890. London was like a wild river, and it was booming. Horse-driven coaches, street trams, construction sites, crowds of people, and—always precisely on an hour—the large sounds of Big Ben as a monumental sound umbrella. The reassurance that the time in the British Empire went as precisely as it always did and always would.

Mise-en-scène

At the Victoria Station, a small crowd dressed in a colorful mix of fine traveling clothes and fashionable afternoon outfits stood in scattered groups, waiting in the cloud of expensive perfumes for the train to arrive. One could safely assume that most of their finery was handmade at tailors, milliners, and shoemakers bearing over their doors the Royal Warrant of Appointment by Her Majesty Queen Victoria.

One of them—a young, elegant gentleman of impeccable appearance—kept looking at his lavishly engraved gold watch. The fob at the end of the fine golden mesh was carved in an extraordinarily colored carnelian. A closer look would show that it bore the image of the god Hermes. This young man was fashionably dressed in a gray-striped afternoon suit with a fine light-brown vest. The expensive gray topper was placed with a slight tilt on his perfectly combed hair. His dark sideburns were shaved to meet under his nose in the form of fine wings. Enveloped in the finest deerskin glove that was the natural tint of pale yellow, his slender hand played with the large ivory knob of his walking stick. The detailed carving depicted a hunting scene. Hidden in the hollow underneath was a long, thin, sharp blade. While waiting, he attracted glances from people standing around him. Alas! They waited too long to get acquainted. The train arrived and stopped with massive clouds of steam and the loud screeching noises of brakes and pistons. All of the compartment doors were pushed wide open with a sharp crack; the sudden explosion of voices made communication almost impossible. The arriving passengers overtook the narrow platform with their overcoats, clumsy traveling handbags, dogs, and children. The collision was inevitable—the pleasant, elegant young gentleman was pushed down to the ground!

There was an immediate commotion, people coming to his rescue, "Now really! How unpleasant! Shocking! Is he hurt?"

Even some of the finest dressed couples rushed to help, and he heard someone say, "Such a darling young man."

It took them several tries to pick up his large-boned body. He smiled apologetically. Finally, he was back on his feet, straightening up his attire. Someone said, "Your top hat, sir—here," and then his, "Ah! Of course. How can I ever thank you enough?"

"Don't mention it," was the response. Then all was well again. The rhythm of this meeting place fell back to its initial meter and noise. Everyone rushed back to their relations. Porters piled all luggage up high on carts, pets were freed from cages and ran around on their colorful leashes. Then some felt it was time to quickly introduce the young, likable gentleman to their female relatives. The London Season was in full swing, after all. They just could not see him now. They started looking around. He was nowhere to be found. Neither were their gold watches, pairs of heavy gold bracelets, nor a pair of ruby earrings.

"Thief!" The echo of their voices suddenly thundered under the iron-and-glass roof of the station. "Robbery! Catch the thief!"

A train leaving from the last platform had just picked up speed. It was heading to the English countryside. A young gentleman in the first-class compartment looked at his gold pocket watch with the engraving of the god Hermes on the carnelian fob. With a smile and deep satisfaction, he turned to the man sitting on his left and said, "On time!"

London! Josef's face finally brightened. He couldn't help it. He felt like a tourist. He wished to become one for at least one day. He didn't want to think. Or worry. "Whatever must come will come anyway," Father used to say. He wished Father could be here. No, Josef must not cry now. He stopped and looked around. He was sick of feeling guilty. He'd done nothing wrong! He'd become a pawn on someone else's capricious game board, and now his life was in danger.

He must return and explain. But to whom? How? Would Baron von Silber be on Josef's side? That was hardly imaginable. A disturbing thought pushed through. Was the baron behind Father's death? Josef felt ill. He wished there was someone close to talk to. Karel. The name felt wrong now. No, that association was done. Mother … the void was painful. Memory works in strange patterns sometimes, and he heard his own voice say, "horror vacui"—the vacuum abhorrence; the long-forgotten term from his short-lived studies of thermodynamics.

Exactly. He was alone. He was in the land of no one. He was frightened and despised himself for that.

Josef looked up at the gray sky. Mother probably was in the south of France.

Josef woke up from his daydreaming. His slightly slanted eyes drifted to a face across the street that, for a second, he thought familiar. He looked again. The face was gone. Nonsense! His desire for being alone was now stronger than giving that another thought. He needed to close his eyes and not think. Why not just enjoy this day?

He crossed the street and climbed inside one of the cabs waiting there.

"Where to, sir?" An unfamiliar sound of Cockney pricked his ears.

"Show me all the great places. Just go!"

The long whip made sharp smacking sounds in the air, and wheels started to rattle on the cobblestones sprinkled with sand. The washed red tassels over the horse's eyes resumed their daily effervescent dance. Annoyed flies hit the air.

Old springs squeaked under the added weight. Sets of short noises held just below the unpleasant level felt like a lullaby. Josef pulled the thick Scottish blanket over his knees and closed his eyes. He was safe.

Karel looked around and felt as if he had never left the Old Continent.

He hadn't expected this. He loved it at first sight. Philadelphia!

"Theater?" was the first that he demanded from the official who welcomed him on the American soil.

"Your name, sir?" demanded the official.

Karel had been preparing for this moment ever since he stepped on the boat. From the moment he saw the newspaper headline in Hamburg, he knew that his only chance to survive was to change his name. At first, his mind was overflowing with names of characters from all the plays he could think of. But then, he thought, if this was his first idea, secret police would think the same. Then one morning on the boat, he leafed randomly through his papers—a small bundle of photographs, letters, and postcards; everything that he could gather in haste before his quick escape. All that remained from his life in Prague. He stared at the postcard his mother gave him. It was the opening night gift of good luck, the "toi, toi, toi" lucky spit for his premiere of Hamlet. She wrote on its reverse. "Never 'Not to be'! Life is the most precious gem we have. You stand on the shoulders of these great people. Because of their determination, you are here now. Remember that. Always. You are the most brilliant star of my life. Toi, toi, toi! Your loving Adele."

After many formalities, way more complicated than Karel could have ever anticipated, the boat slowly moved upstream from one office building to the other up the Delaware River.

It took several unnerving days to reach Philadelphia. Finally, one day, Karel stepped on the shore, perturbed. He looked at his papers and his new name. He repeated it several times to himself to make sure that it flew naturally out of his mouth. He said it out loud at the Philadelphia port, looking the officer straight in the eye. Once he stepped out of the customs building, he pulled out the postcard one more time. Karel examined his ancestors' eyes closely. The fashionable master painter of that time long gone had made them all look smart, important, and untouchable. The famous Bernini who walked the stages of Europe two centuries before him, whose blood ran in his veins. Their image, created by Master painter, became part of his life saving scheme.

He heard his mother's trained voice, the voice of a rare timbre that could reach all the way up to the fourth circle, even with the slightest whisper. "Artists are all cousins, no matter which gifts of art you were given in your cradle. The Muses will always protect you. Just stay faithful to your gifts. Stay humble. Never offend the Muses."

Karel looked down at the points of his shoes through tears. Humble he was not. He did offend the Muses … many times over. Would he ever receive forgiveness? He looked at the postcard one last time. "Thank you."

Karel moved the cherished possession into his breast pocket, climbed up to the landing, and looked around. He wiped his eyes and stepped into the strange new city.

The street in front of him looked familiar. "I am in Europe." He was fascinated by the similarities. After long weeks, he finally smiled again.

"Theater? Teatro? Theater?" he kept asking left and right, but people pointed in different directions.

"Which one are you looking for?" a man asked him in German. Karel thought for a moment, and something occurred to him, something that was not in the equation of his plans. "The German-speaking one? A good one?"

"That will be a problem. The German, I mean. The good ones are right here and all around. Good luck!"

Karel was disappointed. His idea was short-lived.

Instead of saying thank-you, he spat three times over his left shoulder for better luck. The man shook his head and walked away.

Karel kept looking up on the roofs of buildings. He soon located the theater. There it was—the unsightly box hiding the overhead stage space, sitting on the top of the building. Karel crossed the remaining distance with the energy he thought he had left in Hamburg forever.

The name was the Walnut Theater and by the garlands of nuts of that same name, he understood. It was Walnuss in German! He looked at posters. Lillie Langtry was engaged here. He could be Claudius to her Cleopatra; he could be Romeo to her … That memory hurt the worst. He turned and rushed through crowded streets that were shaded by tall buildings. A mix of sorrow, disappointment, anger, and void pushed him forward. He made his way out of the city center without looking where he was going. He did not care. It took him an hour before his pain and madness subdued a little. His emotions were still as raw as a bare nerve, Karel felt unbearably tired. He wanted to curl up right there on the sidewalk. He felt faint. That's when he realized that it had been hours since he'd had something to eat and drink.

He bought a pretzel on the street and dropped into a smoky pub for a pint.

His curiosity started to reemerge. He listened to the background noise of Dutch, some Italian, and French—and then, German again! Perhaps he would not need English that much around this town. Refreshed, with a new jolly spring to his gait, he passed several neat-looking inns and avoided a bunch of dark, dirty-looking ones. It was not until he saw a boarding house with a cleanly swept doorstep, which reminded him of something pleasant and familiar, that he decided to walk in.

The owner was a widow with a little boy still in his cradle. She ran the place with her two unmarried sisters. The trio was the most cheerful congregation Karel had ever seen. They showed him to his quarters, trying to explain everything at once in a mix of English, German, and Dutch, in between their fits of laughter. Once they made sure he loved his room, they left among giggles and private jokes and pokes. Without any strength left in him to make the judgment of whether he would be able to live next to such fireworks of positive emotions, Karel crushed down in the spotless, crisp sheets and fell immediately asleep.

Josef woke up abruptly from his dreamless nap. The cab had stopped suddenly to avoid some kind of collision. It startled him. The pleasant lullaby was over. The buzz of his fear seeped back. Now, the image that he successfully had pushed away for hours came back to annoy his mind.

A strange man had started toward the cab depot at the same moment when Josef was choosing his cab; he looked straight at Josef, hesitated, looked again, and changed direction.

Josef could have sworn that the man recognized him and didn't want Josef to notice. He chose consciously to ignore that face, to step inside the cozy darkness of the cab, and relax.

Now Josef felt his fear closing around his chest again. He knocked on the cab's side. It came immediately to halt.

"Any good beer around here?"

The recommended place was not far from where Josef first hired this cab. It was an inn as well as a busy beer house.

He paid the Cockney and, with his travel bag in his hand, crossed the cobblestone side street. When he entered the busy pub, Josef realized that he'd left his fine gloves in the coach. He hurried back to catch his coachman before any new customer hired him.

He started crossing the street but quickly jumped into the first doorway to hide. The man who'd looked at Josef at the beginning of the day was back. Josef carefully peeked from his hiding place. The stranger, cautiously looking around, was paying the Cockney. Again, glancing briskly around, he then hurried away.

The panic that struck Josef now was paralyzing. He decided to forget about his gloves; instead, he walked toward the great avenues and busy London squares. He kept looking behind him. He had to push himself to stay calm and keep walking. His first instinct was to run, however. He was certain that they'd caught up with him now. In London! He could not believe it. Now he thought of Karel's bright idea. America. It was too late for any regrets. They were quicker than he'd expected. He'd underestimated them. They were after him. The

Imperial Secret Police were notoriously merciless. Josef was sweating and not because he was walking fast.

He walked quicker and quicker, trying not to jog, not to draw attention.

He slowed down, then picked up speed again. Everything he had ever read about spies and the cat-and-mouse game came to his mind. He tried to observe the street around him through shop windows to see if someone suspicious was following him. It was only after he walked through a narrow passage into an elegant square that he relaxed a little. He kept walking randomly around until he was certain there was no one following him there.

Tired and ravenous, he entered what looked like a very respectable pub.

Josef ordered beer and a Cornish pie. He sat down in the dark corner. He ate without enthusiasm and gulped down the full glass of beer. Once he finished, he knew it was time for something much stronger than beer.

The pub was filling up. The noise level reminded Josef of the port of Hamburg. He remembered his father saying, "London is still the safest place in the world." But Josef had his doubts now. He was not certain how to stop his mind from lingering on that strange man paying the cab. Perhaps it had nothing to do with him at all. But his fear was getting louder than the pub.

Josef took a long gulp of whiskey, then one more. After yet another he started feeling a pleasant buzz and, for the first time, he looked around.

The demographic of the place had changed several times while Josef sat there sipping his drinks. Also, several tides from different seas of London society brought and took away curious colors, sounds, and noises as the night progressed. "Here! Whiskey! Encore! Double." Josef's voice tried to reach the man at the counter. No fear, Josef commanded himself. His argument was strong and logical. I am safe here. I look like any of these men at the bar. The pub was overcrowded, even more now, at one o'clock past midnight.

Nobody seemed to hear Josef's order. As he stood up to fetch another whiskey himself, a young man who had entered a few moments ago approached him.

"Whiskey?" he said in a strong accent that engaged Josef right away. "Drrrinks forr eveehryywan!" he called with sure authority. His "r'" rattled back in his throat. Then he looked around with visible pride. Instead of being met with cheers, the crowd of men, too well dressed for such an invitation, seemed to have moved away from where he was standing in his low-class suit. Nobody acknowledged his offer. Josef, who felt the strong need for an uncomplicated human soul, did.

"That is a grand offer! Come and sit with me!" Josef said with a smile, and he pulled up a chair for the young man.

"Knud. Swedish. My mother Denmark," he introduced himself in broken English. Josef pictured all Scandinavians to be tall and broad-faced with red cheeks. Maybe the accent was from somewhere else. The young man couldn't have been more than thirty. He was brown-haired, stout with a small potbelly, and had hands with rough palms. Josef, against all his good manners, did not say his name, but simply pointed to the empty chair. The Scandinavian did not sit down. His excitement made him half stand, half kneel. After a moment he turned the chair around and sat on it as if he'd just mounted a small horse.

"Grahnd day! Knud grahnd day…" With a broad smile, the young man seemed to be in ecstasy. "I rich man now! Today. You know?" He checked Josef's fine clothes with his fingertips without any permission and then pointed at Josef's signet ring. "Aristokrat, ja?" His strong fingers held Josef's fine hand in a tight clutch. He smelled of alcohol and sweat.

Josef felt suddenly uncomfortable. Too polite to send the lad away, he freed his hand and picked up the glass instead. They drank to Knud's sudden fortune, whatever it might be. Yet another gambler, Josef thought with slight disgust. But his memory opened the view of the Riviera and the casino across from the grand hotel where his mother would take them to play. "Just a little," she would say, and they stayed for few short rounds of roulette. Three was her number that she never surpassed. Lose or win, they were out of there and went for a more-or-less opulent dinner at Chez Babette.

A loud toast of "Skål! Cheers!" brought him back from his memory trip.

Between them, Josef and his new companion had many reasons to drink tonight. They drank to luck, to happiness, to Britain, to Queen Victoria, to lucky chance, to the Swedish king, to Denmark … Josef drank away his fear. The new day started behind the stained-glass windows, making the morning look even foggier than it really was.

The small crowd of those who didn't have to go to work became thinner.

Josef was tired, and he went to the loo. When he came back, Knud grabbed his forearm. "Khome wit' me!" He waved his arm, suggesting a faraway place. "Slott!"

Josef did not understand. "Slot? What slot?"

Knud tossed his bag on the green wooden floor and started looking for something inside its deep linen pockets. He located the little stump of a pencil. He flipped over the paper coaster on the table, licked the pencil top, and started drawing a building with turrets. It was a castle. Josef did not understand. What was this young man trying to communicate? "A castle?"

Knud nodded. "Ja, slott. Knud must see …" and he gestured with a stretched arm, almost hitting the man standing close by. "Lång resa. Khome wit' me? Yes?"

Josef's mind was not affected by drinking that much. He understood. "A long trip." He immediately saw the great potential of this accidental meeting. That's it! This is divine intervention. "Deus ex Machina," Father would say; his favorite tool from the ancient Greek theater—the unexpected change of a character's destiny. It sounded perfect. Josef would go away with this jovial traveling Scandinavian lad. They would be like hundreds of tourists this summer. They would hike and see the castle that Knud wanted to see and then more manors and abbeys and parks and whatever. It would be Josef's Grand Tour after all. Brilliant! That would buy him the time he needed for things to calm down in Prague and in Vienna.

After some time, he would go back and clear his name. Then he would be able to connect with people from his father's former cabinet. He would make everything right again. He saw the future clearly now. It was a dreamy scene, lit by a spotlight with yellow and pink filters. Everything was turning into the bright and easy parade of good deeds and lucky reunions, as only the mind of a young man of his age and social standing could produce.

He turned to Knud and said clearly, "Yes."

Knud jumped up enthusiastically and hugged Josef. One more time tonight, his strong physique hiding underneath his simple clothes took Josef by surprise. He pointed at Knud and made a circle in the air. "Family?"

Knud shook his head. "Family?" And without showing any sadness, he explained matter-of-factly. "Död. Jag är ensam. Knud. One." He lifted his index finger.

He was the only one left. Josef noticed a tiny tattoo between the second and third fingers. Instinct made him look away without asking. He put his hand on Knud's arm. "Let's go. I do not like London that much anyway."

Knud picked up his rucksack. He turned to Josef, his simple face full of eagerness. They winked at each other. It looked like genuine camaraderie. Josef was tired of plots and suspicions and felt like giving in to this unexpected offer of friendship. "Which train station?"

Knud searched through his pockets and then read from a small blue-lined piece of green paper. "Victoria Station, London, England."

Traveling in first class was a very comfortable way to sober up.

When Josef finally dropped deeply into his sleep, he had very unsettling dreams. When they arrived in a small town somewhere southwest of London, he couldn't shake off the feeling that somebody had tried to pull his signet ring off his finger while he was asleep. He looked at Knud, who gave him his broad, simple smile and a big yawn. Nonsense, thought Josef, and he felt silly for the moment.

Nevertheless, he checked his wallet and his knife at the first possible moment. All was as before. He touched the secret pocket with money and checks. Nobody can get to those without killing me. He immediately regretted thinking that. That statement brought back the unnerving feeling of fear.

During those long hours on the train, Knud wanted to know everything about Josef. For Josef, it became a fun game of deception. He played it with great bravura. There was one thing he couldn't hide, though. It was the fact that he was a true gentleman with the finest upbringing.

They finally arrived. Tired of listening to Knud's excited broken English for hours, Josef walked up to the first newsboy. He needed to be alone with his own thoughts. "Moment," he said to Knud. He exchanged a few pennies for a thin-looking newspaper. His impatient hands shook the large paper leaves to straighten them up, and he opened the pages.

Time stopped. Josef used all of his inner strength to control his sudden tremble. The photograph on the second page was very blurry. Josef, however, recognized the man. He remembered him from the U Pinkasu pub in Prague. Under the photo, the caption said: "Anarchist Connected to the Prague Murder Shot Dead by Secret Police in Dieppe, France."

Josef's mood of an excited traveler vanished without a trace. "He was innocent!" Josef said out loud in Czech. Like a deafening shot of a firing squad, he heard Baron von Silber's chuckle: "Anarchists? U Pinkasu?"

Knud looked at him. "What?"

Josef realized his mistake. "Nothing." Where his brain used to be was a large bladder. The pressure was unbearable. He closed the page to escape the news and to stop trembling.

"Anarchists Executed for Bombing in Portugal" was the headline on the last page he couldn't avoid seeing. There was a gruesome picture of three young men, tied by ropes to stalks, blindfolded, their bodies in spastic positions left by gunshots. The newspaper artist did not pity those men. He'd sketched them with blood splattered all over them, their faces in the hideous grimace of death.

Josef tried to be calm and rational but with no success. His thoughts were like the roulette wheel. Little boxes, black and white, all spinning in front of his eyes. The man who looked him straight in the face in London. The shot anarchists. The headlines. Sophie–Ann, full of blood. The man's … Stop! Josef commanded himself. His head was about to shatter like a windowpane. The wave of panic made his thighs weak, as if they were hollow as if all of his muscles had atrophied. They are in Dieppe. They are going to find him. They are going to murder him. Nobody will ever know!

He must disappear. He had to go underground and change his identity. Now! At once! Quick! Horse and cart! No, no cart. Nobody must know he was here. He must not leave any footprints.

Josef turned to Knud. His fear came out as nasty, biting impatience. "Where is that bloody castle you want to see? Let's go!"

"Wait, wait! Nej!" Knud tried to slow Josef down. "Mat."

"What do you mean?" Josef could not tolerate any more delays.

Knud waved his hand toward the main street market and made a pinch from his hand, quickly miming eating. "Hunger. Food." He took down his rucksack and pulled out a tin box wrapped in a dirty piece of wax paper. He carefully unfolded the cloth and opened it. Then he took an envelope from the box and pushed it into Josef's hand. "Here."

Josef was irritated but took the letter. He held it with consuming anger. Knud nodded in accord and produced a large, proud smile, commanding cheerfully, "Ja. Read!" Then he added with a boyish skip, "Knud back soon!" And he was off for some provisions.

Josef's fingers tried to calm down. He needed some time to think. He absentmindedly opened the envelope.

"To Mr. Knud Gunnarsson" stated the address.

Josef started walking to escape his mood. His eyes mechanically wandered over the letter as he pulled it out of the envelope. He glanced at the unfamiliar handwriting. It felt as if he was looking at somebody's drawing or an etching. Black and white page. Words and more words. Curves of the meandering calligraphy of somebody's masterful command of penmanship. He started moving his eyes within the waves and arabesques of the black ink, and his eyes got used to them.

Josef stopped. He reread the first paragraph. He felt he needed to sit down. He had to read the paragraph one more time. Then he slowly absorbed the perplexing news.

They were not hiking. They were not about to visit anybody's castle either.

It was Knud who owned that castle, a country manor.

Josef was trying to catalog the information as it was unfolding on the paper in his shaking hand.

There were no servants or any other estate staff present at the moment, wrote the solicitor. He was explaining in great detail everything he thought the new lord of the manor needed to know. Josef's mind was working at the highest speed. He read it all over again.

It evidently had been almost fourteen years since the last family member had died. All the staff was long gone. The park and gardens would need serious care. He would help with new hiring, new planning if the new lord wished. In the end, the solicitor added, "You may enter through the old kitchen. I will leave it open for you. Make yourself at home, sir, and come to see me at your first convenience, please, at…" The address followed. "Besides the sum that I sent to you for your immediate travel expenses, you will receive the full inheritance in money and in shares. I am looking forward to finally meeting you in person. With respect. Yours sincerely…"

Josef's mind stopped spinning as suddenly as it had commenced. A fine thin thread of curious thoughts started unraveling. It got caught on the spindle of Josef's plans.

Knud was back from the market. His canvas rucksack was stuffed with paper packages, and he was holding one more against his chest.

He looked at Josef with the smile of an accomplice. "Prima?"

"Prima," Josef answered absently. His eyes didn't dare to meet Knud's as he took the brown bag from his hands.

Late afternoon sunlight stretched shadows in the park into long dark streams. Josef's head was pounding, a sudden headache slicing his perception apart. Knud's body folded down to the ground. He was dead.

Josef felt faint. He leaned backwards into the branches and slid down. His mind was blacking out.

Everything had happened in quick succession. First, they ate and drank. Then they drank again. Knud asked Josef to take a walk with him. "Kom we see park!" The park must have been very beautiful in the past. It started by the manor as an ornamental French garden and then opened widely into the deceptive free form of an English park, a skillfully, inconspicuously modeled countryside of rolling hills with exotic trees, ponds, and small architectural follies. Josef and Knud crossed the distance quickly before running up the hill. Josef suggested they explore the leafy structure that appeared in front of them. It was even better than he thought. It was a garden maze. They entered.

The silence happened almost immediately. The world out there was muffled by the overgrown yews. There was a strong scent of wet wood; a bright bittersweet smell of grasses crushed under their shoes. Josef felt as if they had entered a different dimension. Everything here had its own laws, over which he had very little control if any at all.

The two young men kept moving forward through the widely spread branches. Their faces were soon full of scratches, but they did not stop, as inner powers inexplicably moved them forward. The ground changed. Grass gave way to pebbles. Another turn in the maze. The black and white pebbles were organized into patterns. Josef looked under his feet, intrigued.

Knud turned. His long knife was pointed at Josef's neck. He stretched his arm and said in fluent English. "First, give me your ring."

Josef didn't move. Knud repeated, with less patience, his voice lowered and barely audible. "The ring, damn it. I don't rob dead bodies."

Josef was finally coming to. The fight had been short and hard. He was still holding the bloody knife, tightly clutched in his palm. Knud's lifeless body, face down, was on the ground that was intricately paved with black and white pebbles. Josef looked up. He was not certain if the noise he'd just heard was there before.

Somewhere close by in the maze, a man's voice suddenly said. "Anybody there? I am lost! Help me!"

Josef held his breath and tried to decide his next move. The voice was coming slowly closer and closer. The unknown man's feet were making crunching sounds on the pebbles. Josef slid forward behind the first wall of plants and pressed his body against the old yews. His body was still shaking from the fight and loss of blood. Now, the steps stopped. He heard a muffled shout. The man had found the dead body. Then silence.

Josef waited, his breath pulled in, his body stretched like a bowstring, his stomach sucked in so that it almost touched his spine. His fingers, squeezed to the breaking point, still clutched the knife. He listened. The short silence was suddenly replaced by a strange clicking noise. Josef recognized the sound. He too had been an avid photographer. He opened some of his fingers that were holding the knife to relieve the spasm. Then he clutched it even tighter. His analytical mind finally started working. He ran a quick succession of facts and summed up his situation. If the photos got to the police now, then Josef would not be able to assume his new identity. They would certainly come here; they would start investigating. They would find out all about him. They would accuse him of murder. Of two murders.

He heard a new type of noise. The accidental witness was now trying to find his way out of this maze. Josef knew that he needed to get that film.

His body exhausted, weak in his knees, Josef started following the noise in the maze. He leaned against the old shrubs for support. The noises the accidental witness was making became frantic. Josef became frantic.

He heard the man's quick breath ending in short wheezing. He tried to find where the man had gone. Suddenly, there was a loud rustling. Josef heard the thud as the man's body fell somewhere on the grass. His fall was followed by a short swear word spat out in pain and then the dull noise of quick, heavy steps. They became less and less audible. Josef charged quickly in that direction. He made a strong attack on the green wall with his full body weight. It gave in. He rolled out on the other side, scratched all over his face and neck. He was hissing in pain, trying to wipe his scratched, sweaty, bleeding face. He looked around. There, almost on the top of the next hill, was the photographer, running away with all of his strength.

Josef tucked his chin down and started jogging. He realized that they were running toward the river. His mind began creating a new scenario. Josef's hands were sweating. He had to use his arms to pick up speed. He focused on his moves. A large stroke, another, and one mo—the knife slid from his hand and dropped somewhere in the grass. Josef's body almost fell from the abrupt stop he made. He reached for the knife and saw Knud's blood.

A projectile vomit tossed him down to his knees. He barely heard the train whistle from the opposite side beyond the woods. Josef looked up. He wiped his mouth. Still spitting bile all around in the grass, he tried to stand up. The photographer was gone. Then, only for a second, Josef noticed him among the trees on the slope. There was a shortcut to the train station. The man must have been here before. This was Josef's last chance. In quick succession, he ran across the meadow and then up through the forest. He passed centuries-old stone markings, heralding that he had just crossed into the neighboring county.

Up, on the road, he saw the man not far in front of him. The man turned and looked at Josef. In what seemed to Josef like a new burst of energy, he started toward the station. Josef kept running. His long legs got into the rhythm again. Up the hill and one more curve. Less than a mile in front of them was the station. Josef started humming the beat of his steps, puffing the short sounds through his nose. He could see the man with his camera was much closer. He was making the last curve toward the train station. Josef kept running. He started catching up with the photographer and realized how close to the station they were already. He tried to quickly decide what to do at such an exposed place, and he slowed down a little. Then, the unexpected happened.

The man stopped. Josef stopped. The man turned and pointed his camera lens at a stunned Josef and took his picture. Then he turned to run away with his precious catch.

What followed next was one of those supernatural achievements that happen under life-threatening circumstances, and then you read about them with awe in newspapers. Using his momentum, Josef tossed his body forward and crossed the distance between him and the man in a flash.

He dropped with full weight on the photographer and stabbed him, killing him instantly. The collision tossed Josef to the side, and he fell on the dusty ground. Hurting, his blood mixed with sweat and dust, Josef lay there, waiting for his energy to return. A sudden movement behind the garden fence at the station caught Josef's attention. With a remnant of his strength, he rolled off the road into the ditch. Hidden behind short, half-dried shrubs growing in the sandy soil, he waited, motionless. The field road was warm and fragrant in the late afternoon sun. Josef was getting ready for the man who was running here. The fragrance of dry grasses mixed with Josef's sweat. Low dust sprinkles shot from under the man's shoes, leaving the dust cloud behind as he got closer. He surely must have seen the previous scene. Josef reached for his pocket knife and tried to shift into a better position. The man was now a few feet away from Josef. Josef tried to activate his tired senses; his muscles were getting ready for the attack.

With disgust and relief at the same time, Josef watched as the well-dressed young gentleman stopped, and knelt down by the photographer's body. His well-manicured fingers ran through the dead man's pockets and stole everything he found there. Josef's first reaction was to jump up and smack that immoral bastard and take him to the police station. He remained motionless until the thief stood up and started back toward the station. The man completely ignored the small camera that the dead man was still holding in his hands. Josef was safe. Only now he allowed his exhausted body to turn on its back, and for a second he closed his eyes. A whistle from the small station announced the leaving train.

At that instant, Josef heard the noise of long steps jogging quickly back toward him. It was too late to move. Josef froze. The young man made one rapid movement. Josef hadn't expected that. He had no time to react.

The thief bent and grabbed the camera from the dead man's hands. He ran with large strides back to the station, holding the small box that contained the crucial roll of film tightly in his hand. He was gone.

Josef fell back on the warm sandy ground, rolled to the ditch, and started to cry.

The thief jumped with bravura onto the already moving train and slammed the door of the first-class compartment behind him. He dropped deeply into the cushioned green-velvet seat. As the train moved out of the station, he pulled out his gold pocket watch. Holding the soft gold mesh with the carnelian fob with the carving of Hermes, the god of thieves, the elegantly dressed gentlemen smiled and said aloud with great satisfaction, "On time!"

ACT THREE

London, 1953

The little bell placed above the door that never properly closed rang in its low pitch. Then again, and again, and one more time, as the customer who just entered played with it, swinging it in and out.

When he stopped, his brown eyes observed the space through the rectangle he'd formed between his thumbs and index fingers. There was a simple wedding band on his left hand.

A young woman appeared from the back of this old antique shop. Adam turned and placed her image in the golden cut of his hand frame.

Martha's dress flattered her figure. It was her own copy of the one she's seen in the last year 1952 Vogue magazine. The heavy silk material blended perfectly with the Louis XVI furniture. It was multiplied by mirrors and glass display cases as she came closer to Adam. "What can I do for you, sir?" Her deep green eyes darkened one hue as she smiled at him.

"I am not sure. I was just walking by and thought there could be something for me in here."

Martha moved toward a curio cabinet. "A silver candlestick, perhaps? Or ..." She thought slowly and then said, "An inlaid Damascene saber?"

"I thought maybe something more fun." Adam stirred her attempts. "A chaise-longue?"

A smile kept twinkling in her eyes. "That's a thought!"

"I see a perfect one over there." Adam stepped toward Martha, his arms opening wide as he started approaching her. She was quick. Before he knew it, she was already stepping among the Persian carpets from the other side. "Not so quickly, sir!"

But Adam was quick too. He caught her around her tiny waist. Martha rolled out of his arms and, giggling, tossed some cushions under his feet. Then, still walking around with quick steps, she reached for a small box and placed it quickly in her lover's surprised hands.

"An old camera, perhaps? Sir is a professional; I can tell!"

They both could barely speak as their giggles came in gusts while they kept moving through familiar space, playing their favorite game.

"It's a rare piece!" she shouted while laughing and trying to escape her lover. "The famous little handheld!"

But he was not easily impressed, not even in their foreplay. "Rare? Ha! There are hundreds of those! I want something better."

Adam leaned forward and pressed the small box back into Martha's hands. Her head moved quickly to the side before his lips realized the kiss with which he planned to end their game. Her body slid out of his reach.

"Not rare?" She pretended to be shocked and devastated. Hardly controlling her laugh, she raised her voice. "Oh dear, sir. I beg you; do not leave!" Her voice mimicked the famous theater actress they both loved. "I will sing for you. Or dance for you." Her eyebrows raised in a question mark. "How's that?"

"All the above! Deal!" shouted Adam and noisily landed on one of the upholstered sofas.

"Careful there!" Martha's professional side came to life for a second, but then her lover's apologetic face made her laugh. She assumed a seductive pose, copying an Italian movie star she'd seen in the film magazines. Then she called out loud "Rumba!"

She lifted her arms. Adam saw the contour of her figure; he thought of how amazing it was that this young, exciting woman belonged to him. In only a few minutes, he would kiss her, and, as every day, she would close the store. They would run upstairs and make love until there was not a single drop of strength in their bodies or in the day behind the narrow windows. Martha started singing with a comically exaggerated voice.

She was mixing Spanish and Portuguese the way she heard it on the radio. Using the small camera as percussion she started shaking it in the rhythm of her little song. Adam jumped up. "Can't you hear that?" He was furious.

Martha stopped, confused. She didn't recognize the face of the man in front of her. "Hear what? What is wrong, Adam?"

Her arms left an invisible elegant line in the air. Her performance was over. Martha looked at Adam and didn't know what to say.

"Can't you?" he demanded. His unexpectedly rude impatience made her angry. She remained silent. He pulled the camera from her hand with the force she never would have associated with him. "There's a roll of film in it. Can't you hear that?"

Martha's late-afternoon mood lay all around them, shattered into pieces. She felt like adding some more. Maybe a vase or two?

Adam was now carefully shaking the camera by his ear. Martha realized that she had ceased to exist for him. With the voice of a young archeologist looking into a tomb full of gold, Adam gasped and repeated, "There is a forgotten film in it ... Can you hear? This is amazing! There is still a roll of film." He knew that he'd overreacted. To save face—and this afternoon—he changed his tone to an enthusiastic invitation. "Let's go to my studio! We'll develop it together."

"You go and develop it, darling." Martha's effort was just a courtesy to their love. "That's fine. I will wait here ... for my ... hero."

Adam missed the irony and, without kissing her, rushed out the door. It made an unusually strong attempt to close behind him.

Adam felt the heat above his stomach as if he'd had too much to drink. His brain expanded to the point of bursting. His face was tingling. He could not decide what to do next.

When he started developing the film earlier that afternoon, at first all of his enthusiasm cooled off. He was disappointed and angry. He was angry with himself. So this was why he interrupted his perfect afternoon with Martha—a collection of half-century-old photographs from the English countryside!

Swell! Small picturesque stations, neat country cottages, little shop fronts. Some climbing roses, hedges, and park vistas. Lakes with architectural structures. Country manors. Bored out of his wits, he watched the next batch of photos coming to life in the chemical bath—a man, lying facedown on a black-and-white pattern of pebbles.

Adam looked again. He was not mistaken. There was a man lying facedown on the pebbles, dead. His blood-soaked white shirt was torn where a knife had stabbed him from the back.

Adam picked up the phone to call Martha, but once the operator asked him what number he wished to call, Adam hung up.

He sat down with the photos in his hands. Over and over again, with a strange, insatiable fascination, he kept looking at them, turning them, and looking at them again from different angles. He tried to organize his thoughts.

Adam was not sure what to do. He felt very protective of these photographs. This is what scientists must feel when they discover something revolutionary, he thought. Adam felt passionate and almost obsessive about his discovery.

This was not revolutionary, and there was no Nobel Prize in the end. This was a murdered body. A photo report of a murder over fifty years delayed.

There was only one person he had to talk to now—Robert. That was it! He would call his old colleague. Adam knew from the papers that Robert had become the superintendent by now. His word should give Adam what he needed—permission to research the police archives.

The meeting was warmer than Adam anticipated. They'd worked together at one point, but that was before the Second World War.

Robert, now stouter than Adam remembered him, also had gained some joviality. "Adam! It's been ages!" Without giving Adam any space for a reply, he continued with all of the authority that allowed him to climb up social ladders. "Married? Do I know her?"

Adam reached for his wallet and pulled out a small snapshot of his wife.

"I'll be darned! Rose? Wasn't she your family ward or something like that?"

Adam opened his mouth to answer. Too soon.

"Isn't she too young for you? Children?" The superintendent suddenly slapped his thighs and chuckled loudly. This was the Robert that Adam wished to avoid.

"Oh, my poor little Adam! Slow as always, and I am not making it easy! Now, what brings you here?"

Adam had two choices. He reminded himself why he'd come here, and he chose to stay. "To answer in order of what you asked: yes, no, and no."

The superintendent laughed through his nose and hugged Adam, almost lifting him off the floor. In defense arts, he was always the best one in the academy. Adam's spine gave some dull rattling sounds.

"Robert, I do not do jujitsu anymore. I am just a photographer." And he twisted his body out of Robert's arms.

"And still modest! I remember well," commented the superintendent and then added, "I have been following your work for years. You made a very good name for yourself." Adam was flattered. He hadn't expected Robert to know anything about him. "The Rembrandt of Photographic Lens!" Robert quoted one review's headlines.

"Such a silly wordplay with my last name..." Adam was not in the mood for conversations about his artwork now. "I need your help, Robert."

Robert looked up at Adam without expression, but before his thoughts could proceed with the scenario of another old friend asking for money, Adam added, "There was a murder."

Robert was all attention. In moments he was fully interested—no jokes, no irony. "A murdered body, fifty years ago? I'll be darned. You developed all of the photos, I presume."

"Still drying out." Adam was hardly capable of explaining everything.

His brain was quicker than his tongue, and he stuttered over a few words before calming down. This had not happened to him since he was a boy. He was so excited that he forgot to feel upset. Adam unfolded his findings in front of an intrigued Robert. He had the list of country train stations. He meticulously wrote down all the names from the previous photographs. "Evidently, someone found the body, photographed it, and then—"

"Left the film in the camera." Robert finished Adam's sentence. "And forgot about it? How odd."

Adam saw the inspector's growing interest. "Precisely."

"Any other pictures after that one?"

Adam felt the rush in his brain. "Well, yes. There is one more. It looks like someone's figure."

Robert looked up. "And?"

Adam shook his head "The very first portable camera … not a chance. It is only a blur. Just a shadow … nothing more."

The superintendent made a small gesture, illustrating the insignificance of that information. "Well, well, well … how very odd. Let's look into some long-forgotten reports of murdered reporters, private investigators …"

"Photographers," added Adam, his obvious first choice.

Robert thought for a moment and then picked up the phone.

In a matter of minutes, Adam had his permit.

"Report back!" hollered the superintendent, but Adam was too quick. His reply came from afar, muffled by the noises of the police headquarters.

Police archives were, in fact, next door, just a different part of this complex on the Victoria Embankment. Adam always found it very amusing that police headquarters were two of the jolliest-looking buildings in London. The bright red brick facade with horizontal white stripes connecting all windows, two round towers on its corners, Renaissance-like porticoes, gray slate roof with playful mansards, and tall candylike red-and-white striped chimneys. Adam smiled. What a monument to the Victorians!

The atmosphere in the archives was one of a study. Quiet and slow.

The officer at the helm of this space was an old, patient man, past his retirement, impeccably dressed in a police uniform. Adam told him the story. The man's face lit up. Adam's trained eye saw the handsome features of a heartbreaker.

He led Adam through the maze of shelves, his highly polished shoes making short squeaky sounds. He finally pointed to the section that, as Adam and Robert deduced, should bring some tangible results. Adam had to climb the wooden ladder several times to get down the files he needed. The atmosphere of time standing still took Adam's thoughts far away from the documents he was looking through. It was as if his movement through the still air, smelling of old paper, dust, and tobacco was a gate to another dimension. His movements slowed down, and with time on his hands, he did not fight it but allowed the movie retrospective to move slowly, frame by frame …

…The war had ended. Life was gradually coming back to its regular rhythm.

Too much had happened, and Adam was aware that going back to his job in the police force, photographing dead bodies, was not an option for him anymore. When the war started, he'd been drafted as a war photo correspondent, something he thought would make sense of his profession under the circumstances. After he saw his comrade shredded by a hand grenade, Adam tossed his camera and ran to help the poor guy. There, he suddenly understood that he couldn't do photo reporting. He drove the ambulance for the rest of the war and swore to never again look at one more bloody corpse in his life. In 1946 he opened his own portrait studio. London was rising from her ashes. He chose a fashionable quarter of the town. He was done with the lower middle class. His ambitions were larger than those of his father. His work started getting attention. His portraits became popular within some highly fashionable crowds in Mayfair and Notting Hill. Some even made it into a few respectable art publications. His days were divided between his studio and his old widowed father. One day, however, he'd had enough of it all.

Adam decided to see things that he had been just passing in his hectic life. He wanted to see his neighborhood in a close-up. He walked around and ended in that little antique store that he passed by bus every day. He always admired its marquee hanging over the door. It looked as if they'd left it there from times when Oscar Wilde used to stop by. Martha ran the store with her father at that time.

The slightly sunken space smelled of old wood, wicker, brass, and beeswax. When this thirtysomething young woman appeared from the back of the store, Adam couldn't conceal his excitement.

Martha always looked as if she had freshly washed her face. Her high cheekbones and small, straight nose full of delicate freckles made her deep green eyes look larger. With dark rims around her green irises, her eyes resembled the Faberge malachite jewelry box at her shop window. Adam couldn't imagine ever leaving her side from that first day. Like so many of their generation, they would say with sad anger, "Hitler took the best years of our lives." They promised themselves to bring them all back.

Martha would smile at Adam, slightly tilting her head. Her Titian curls would drop over her mouth. She would not brush them away. He would pick them up between his lips.

They would make love everywhere. All spaces, all surfaces at his studio, and at his home were theirs. Martha would go home after their lovemaking without taking a shower. Not even washing her face. She loved putting her nose into the bend of her elbow to find Adam's sweet smell there for the rest of the day. Sometimes, while walking home, when nobody was around, she would make an extreme movement with her lips, moving them up in an uneven pout close to her nose, so that she could smell the skin around her lips, still holding the scent of Adam's sex. After she arrived home, she would rush upstairs to be alone for a few more moments with the memory of Adam's body.

Adam wanted to marry Martha from the day they met, but she wasn't ready to marry. Maybe it was the war that made her feel the need for absolute freedom at the moment; maybe she didn't want to repeat her late mother's mistake. Then Rose happened. Adam never asked Martha again.

The applause was a balm. Vaudeville in Philadelphia was not Shakespeare in the National, but Karel was back on the stage. That was all that mattered.

During his second month of performing anything they gave him, one night he noticed a man watching him. He appeared after the performance started and stood at the same spot for the next four days. By now, Karel almost forgot why he'd come to America. His fear returned. On the fifth day, he did not go straight backstage but mixed in with the audience, looking for the man. He was already there. Karel saw him talking to the usher. He saw him paying some banknotes to him. Karel felt sick out of panic. He decided not to go on the stage that night.

As he turned to leave, the usher recognized him and waved. There was no way out. "You lucky bastard!" The usher called to him with a broad smile lacking a few teeth. "It's Mr. Bonafeaux, director of the Chestnut Theater. He's been fishing for new talent. Brace yourself; he wants you to stop in his office tomorrow at noon."

And his left hand gave Karel the jovial slap of a lumberjack. The pain took away Karel's relieved smile. He thought for a moment what the usher's right-hand slap must have been when the right arm was still there.

Karel let the applause pour over him like a liniment. Laughter made him drunk on happiness. Gasps from the audience in times of the stage fight, their screams of surprise watching physical tricks—that felt like opium. He could not have enough of that. Ever. It was a drug, the most fantastic fantasy realizing itself in actual time, while he was in its center—not as an observer, but the active agent making all that happen.

Karel did all of that so well. Effortlessly. Audiences adored the young, handsome actor. More and more crowds were drawn to see him at the Chestnut Theater in Philadelphia.

It did not take long before Mr. Bonafeaux sent for him. He handed him a stack of banknotes and pushed some into his pockets.

"You are a great success, as I predicted. I have big plans for you, young man." His hands suggested a large font on a poster. "A grand American tour." He paused and prepared to play his ace. "And then"—he made one more dramatic pause and turned his gleaming face to Karel—"Europe!"

There was dead silence. But experienced Mr. Bonafeaux knew that Karel's silence was an odd reaction of a young man whose golden future just unexpectedly opened in front of him. Dumbfounded, Karel stood there, staring straight ahead. Mr. Bonafeaux chuckled and puffed from his cigar. His protégé looked as if he'd been struck by lightning. "That's all right, my friend. We'll talk more tomorrow. Come here around noon."

Karel never saw Mr. Bonafeaux again.

Adam closed the last of the police archival materials and folded all of his notes. He scribbled an address on a small piece of paper he'd torn from the notebook that the "heartbreaker" had offered him a few hours ago. His search here was done.

Back on London's busy street, Adam decided not to take the tube but instead to enjoy the ride from a bus. The double-decker took him to places where he would not venture otherwise. Although perfectly respectable, he felt that he'd made a definite move to the higher layer of society than the one living around here.

He jumped from the platform of the red bus the second it stopped, almost trampling the conductor. Now he could not wait to cross the street. London traffic was dense here at this hour. He was quick to cross and laughed off angry, obscene gestures a few cab drivers sent after him.

The side street of pleasant appearance, spared during the Blitz, ended in a small park. Number twenty-three was the corner townhouse, reflecting old, tall, grown trees in all of its windows.

Adam rang the bell. His pulse was still racing from his quick walk. He held in his breath in anticipation of a miracle. There was no sound coming from the house. He exhaled and rang one more time. This time he held down the slowly chiming bell impolitely for a long time.

Only one window was ajar in the whole facade. What a waste of such a perfect day, he thought. Summer was almost gone. The jingling sound of the key from the other side of the door made him stand upright.

An old woman in a simple gray-and-cream polka dot dress appeared in front of Adam with a question on her face. Her white lace collar, a small Victorian lover's knot pin, and spotless cuffs were a reminder of her youth. Adam briefly introduced himself and handed her both the superintendent's permit and his calling card. She recognized Adam's name from magazines.

"How can I help you, Mr. Brandt?" Her voice was soft and friendly. Her unusually young-looking hands caught a few streams of her almost-white hair and smoothed them back behind her ear. She had fine features and very lively gray eyes. Adam was careful not to scare her in any way. She was the only person who could have any supporting evidence or any information about the photographs. She was the one hope Adam had. A widow of the only murdered person in the large area somewhere north of the maze with black and white pebbles. The countryside from which Adam compiled the photos.

The murder had happened about fifty years ago. It was a theft murder. The murderer was never caught. Insufficient evidence. Case closed. Everything was stolen from that poor man.

"Insufficient evidence" was what intrigued Adam in this old case.

Now, he stood here with hope. Somehow, Adam felt that this woman was the key to his mystery. Who was the photographer? Where did he take the photo of the unknown murdered man, lying with a deadly wound in his back on intricate patterns of black and white pebbles? In Adam's opinion, the names of stations and manors that the unknown camera owner took were not any type of private investigation. It all looked like a selection ... a compilation for a collection for ... what? Maybe someone had hired this unknown man to create a visual path through that part of England. He found a dead body ... and then ... what? Got scared and exited the project? Tossed the camera? No, a photographer never would have done that. Did someone steal that camera?

"Do come in. It's been a long time since I spoke about..." She hesitated, looking for a word. She did not find it at that moment. "Tea?"

They sat down in a lovely, bright drawing-room, and Adam waited until she was ready to talk about the tragedy.

"He was murdered by a thief, you know. Poor Max."

Adam broke the promise he'd made to himself and asked quickly. "Was he a photographer?"

"Max?" The old lady made a long pause. She looked far away, and a delicate, faint smile illuminated her features. It was an echo of a memory, and Adam could not decide if she was bluffing when she said, "No ... oh no..."

She took a sip from her tea and placed it back on the table, wiping her lips with a fine linen napkin embroidered with daisies.

"I was just twenty-three when he died. He was an older man, you know. He was not into any novelties. He was very ... very ... Victorian," she concluded, not giving her statement any deeper thought. "I got rid of everything right before I remarried." She reached for her cup again.

Adam understood. "Of course." He held his cup, frozen halfway toward his lips. His spirit sank. Then there was really nothing to talk about. He felt the void filling up this room, overflowing into the afternoon.

What did he expect? A shrine to the deceased with an intact dark room stuffed with photographs that would unfold the mystery? He felt the anger pushing into his veins where there had been his enthusiasm a few moments ago. His tea unfinished, he stood up, trying very hard not to show his disappointment.

"Thank you for the tea and your time."

They walked through the half-lit spotless hallway. Everything here was neatly organized. Even the umbrellas in the brass holder by the door were standing at attention. In his mind, Adam saw a military officer carrying a young woman in her wedding dress over the doorstep, into this house. New life, new family. The old case was closed. She showed him out.

Once on the street, Adam needed some moments to think.

He crossed to the small park and sat down on the first bench. Its dark wooden back support radiated the heat of the sunny afternoon but Adam paid no attention today.

That's it then, he thought. There is no case. Max was the only logical link. Or could have been … if only. Only that he was not a photographer.

"Case closed." He already heard Robert's voice in his mind, and he hated Robert, he hated himself, and he hated all of London.

"Mr. Brandt! Hullo, Mr. Brandt!"

Adam tried to smile as he crossed the street toward the old lady who was waving at him now.

"I forgot," she said softly with an apology. "Max's hunting jacket is in the attic." She pointed upstairs. "I hung it up there when they brought it from … from …" Even after all those decades, she was not able to say it out loud.

"From the morgue?" Adam asked quietly.

"Yes," she whispered.

Adam carefully unwrapped the jacket from the brown paper full of old police stamps. He didn't feel any enthusiasm. He'd returned because he felt he owed it to the woman downstairs who so politely had allowed him into the horror of her past.

It was hot up here. He had to take off his jacket and unbutton his shirt. Pigeons were trotting loudly on the roof tiles, their bubbly voices sounding out their never-ending repetition of the love call. Sun was warming the wooden beams, and they gave out the honey-like scent that reminded him when, as a boy, he used to play in the attic … "Father! Damn." Adam had forgotten. Yet again. Rose had told him yesterday that Father got a little talkative in a strange kind of way. The nurse asked for him to come around today. He'd go there later today, then.

Now, he thought, what have we here? Adam made himself take the shooting jacket down from the hanger. He was looking at it without any interest. He'd seen many of them in his life. He lifted it, ready to hang it back.

Suddenly, it occurred to him that there was something odd about this one, but he could not pinpoint what it was. He spun the jacket slowly in his fingers. Just another dead end; he felt he was wasting time. Only out of his professional habit did he try to visualize the shooting jackets as he'd seen them when he was young. Between the wars, he would join friends for a chase in the country. He knelt down now, closed one eye as if looking through his lens, and narrowed the other. There they were, all intact in his professional memory.

The small crowd in hunting attire. I need more detail. Adam tried to focus his brain as if it was his lens. He blinked his eyes and then looked again. There! He looked back at the jacket. He saw it now. The leather on the shoulder was not used. It had no patina whatsoever that a gun would have left. This might be called a hunting jacket, but Adam was certain that it had never seen any actual shooting.

In a flash, Adam ran his hands through all eight pockets. Nothing. Except for hard crumbs half a century in the making, nothing. This jacket was just a pretense, a screen to cover something else … to cover what?

An affair, perhaps? Another woman. He shook his head. Yes, that must be it. How easy to say to your young, inexperienced wife,

"I'm going shooting in the country." A wave of guilt mixed with annoyance ran through his stomach.

He put the jacket back on the hanger and then, without care, hung it back. Adam was hot. The stuffy, intense scent of the wooden beams was choking him. The dry heat was filling the attic, pushing all air out underneath the red tiles. Whatever was this jacket's secret, it was not for Adam to find. In the most annoying sync, the heat and his impatience reached their peaks.

Adam bent down to pick up the stamped brown paper and looked up, thinking already about his father's progressing illness. Sunlight moved in its path a few millimeters further, just enough to hit the jacket from a new angle. All the stitches and patches, folds, and buttons were now an exact, sharp bas-relief.

Adam stood up, eyes fixed on one spot in the fabric. His heart was beating in his throat so loudly that he feared it must be resonating throughout the whole house. There, on the edge of the jacket, way below the right pocket, the afternoon sunlight brought up a small, bulky form.

Adam recognized the shape immediately. It was a roll of film. Through a small hole in the fold of the lining, it had dropped into its hiding place and stayed undetected for decades. The shooting jacket! Adam smiled at the joke and tipped his hat to Max, his late unknown colleague.

He had to make the hole a little larger to get through to the film. As he pushed, the lining gave way, and all the coats and jackets fell down, knocking over all other old, forgotten objects as well.

"Are you all right?" shouted Max's wife from downstairs.

"I'm fine. Not to worry." Adam's voice sounded out like a melody.

He was back down with her in a few moments. "I just pressed too hard and all came down. Sorry. I replaced it as it was," he said apologetically.

"Oh, do not worry. Nobody ever goes up there. Nothing, right?" asked the old woman, her face looking younger in the honey-colored reflection of sunlight now bouncing off the polished wooden floor.

Adam looked into her young-looking eyes and smiled tenderly. "Nothing"

The applause felt like ... no, this was not applause. Karel woke up, his body hurting from the second-class seat. The steam train, making hissing noises, was pulling under the huge roof. Karel clearly heard someone shout, "Central Station!" His decision to go to New York after Philadelphia looked like the best at the moment. The theater was dangerous ground for him. His talents were undisputed and came forward in an instant, wherever and whatever he played. He had to make a painful, thick line behind that life from now on. He was not prepared for it, but it was a question of life or death.

If Philadelphia was still a bit like Amsterdam, New York was like nothing he'd seen before. The noise of the city was unbearable. Everything and everyone were constantly on the move—people, coaches, a few new vehicles, streetcars, horses, and carts. He walked through lower Manhattan, hoping to find "For Hire" signs. After one beer and walking too long, he took the Metropolitan across to what they called Brooklyn. A new terminal had just opened, and Karel decided to see all of New York.

He could not find anything appealing about that place and walked back across the bridge. He stopped and stared across the water at the new Statue of Liberty—a tall, statuesque woman draped in a stola. Enlightening! He thought of his mother in her role as Titania in A Midsummer Night's Dream, his mother as Cleopatra, as Mary, Queen of Scots ... He heard her voice. He would never see her again. He would never hold her face of Juliet in his palms, whispering close to her lips the passionate words of his Romeo. Mother. He really never called her that, as everybody always called her by her first name. She was very young when he was born, and she never corrected him when he called her Adele. He longed to kiss her sweet face that never knew frowns when he was around. How deeply he had hurt her!

Down a long way under him were dark waves, splashing and moving, as if it was a pot of boiling water. He stared, fascinated, through the iron railing to the depths. He was reminded of the bridge and the shallow river underneath when they were leaving Prague. It would have been certain death, had he jumped. The water under the Brooklyn Bridge was magical and magnetic. But the actor in Karel was already observing him at the same time as he was looking down. He tried to remember and store away all of the emotions that rushed through his body at that very moment. He recalled what his mother, Adele, had told him about her youth when she got caught in Paris in 1871 during the Prussian War. How she saw an officer killing a young boy who was tossing mud at soldiers; how the little boy's mother collapsed on her child's dead body; and how Adele, instead of covering her face or running away, stood there, observing every reaction, every emotion of the desperate, devastated, heartbroken mother. Years later, her Clytemnestra, the tragic mother of Iphigenia in Aulis, the classical Greek drama, was born with almost inhuman force from that experience, taking major theaters of Europe by storm.

It was late. Hunger reminded Karel that he was still alive. He crossed to Manhattan and tried to find a place to have an inexpensive lunch and a pint.

He turned into a short back alley, walking toward the place that someone on the street just recommended to him. Before he could find it, the back door of a pub flew open, and a string of German swear words accompanied a young man, who ran out and quickly disappeared around the corner. A stout man with a head full of blond-almost-white hair rushed out but then waved his hand, still holding a red checkered kitchen towel. He looked straight at Karel. "Sprichst du Deutsch?"

Karel was hungry. Here was a chance not to touch his money. He made a quick decision. He looked at the man and nodded. "Ja. Ich spreche Deutsch."

—ων—

Martha was sitting on the couch, reading. She heard Adam's key and ran through the long hallway to meet him. She'd already forgiven him for everything. She made him the center of her existence. He would always come back to her.

Their quarrels came and went. Their separations were filled with exciting, unbearable longing. Their passionate welcomes had not lost anything since the force of the first day.

They collided in a storm of sighs, shouts, and monumental fragments of gestures, pulling off pieces of clothing, reaching into their nakedness for touches, kisses, caresses, passionate bites, dropping to their knees on the long runner, rolling onto the Persian ornaments, and always trying to ignore the speed of time that would separate them again too soon.

Martha was everything that Rose was not. Now, she was sleeping on Adam's chest. From the hallway floor, they moved to the sofa in the drawing-room.

He blew off her red curl from underneath his nose, where it tickled. It swung back. He moved his head a little higher.

Adam thought of Rose's long dark hair. The hair of a young girl, silky and obedient. He could not imagine taking Rose with crushing force into his arms, or biting her shoulders, leaving red-blue bruises. Martha wore them proudly for days, looking down secretly on the exciting reminder of her furtive coexistence with Adam.

Adam could not imagine raising his voice at Rose. It was unthinkable that Rose would ever use a loud voice in any argument with anybody. Hers was logical; she was pleasant and quiet. Her relationships were almost entirely devoid of grand emotions and gestures. She was always tactful and soft-spoken. Rose was like a kitten. Adam smiled. She would come when she pleased and sat on his knees. Ever since he could remember, she'd sat on his knees.

As a very little girl, when he was a young man, he would pick her up, put her on his knees, and they would play the ancient baby game, "This Is the Way the Cavaliers Ride." She was already giggling long before he got to the part when he let her fall through his suddenly parted thighs toward the floor. She couldn't wait for that surprising drop! Rose knew that he would always catch her. Her trust in him was complete. She had never tired of that game. Rose never knew that her parents made her Adam's ward long before the war in Europe became reality again.

When Adam returned from the front, first he heard that they all perished in the Blitz. Then a letter arrived for him from a lawyer.

Adam didn't know what to do first. Then he picked up his hat and left for the countryside, where groups of London children were still living so-called happier, safer lives.

He found the orphanage. Rose was coming down the stairs, three dolls in her arms—they were her whole remaining world.

She'd named them with her mother. She would never say "my late mother."

They were named after famous ballerinas. Maria, for Taglioni; Anna, for Pavlova; and Margot, after the new star at Old Vic. She saw Adam, dropped her dolls, and ran into his arms.

Adam took her hand and brought Rose into his life.

"Adam?" Martha woke up and was looking at him suspiciously from beneath. "Is everything all right?"

He sat up. "Come, I'll show you something."

A few minutes later, they were sipping red wine, and she was sitting on his knees.

He absentmindedly kissed her shoulder. "You see, the jacket was never used." His fingers rolled the unused film on the coffee table in front of them.

"Yes? What does that mean?" She was confused but did not want to start an argument.

"In my opinion, that means that Max was a photographer. The shooting jacket was just a joke he played on the outside world. He went 'shooting,' the manly sport to do in his old-fashioned mind. But instead, he went shooting pictures from a camera that nobody knew he owned."

"But that's just your own theory, isn't it? Maybe someone from his shooting party just asked him to hold on to a new roll of film." Martha kissed Adam's neck "You don't have any connecting evidence? Do you?"

Adam stood up abruptly. Martha slipped skillfully into the other chair, preventing her fall.

"No, I do not." Adam was surprised by the tone of his own voice and added in a much softer manner, "I have none." He looked out the window, playing with the large pink and green tassel hanging on this side of the heavy curtain. "I am sure now that, for Robert, this will not be a reason to continue. Another roll of an unused film. This proves nothing. The old case is closed." He threw the tassel with all of his disappointment in the air, and it started twirling on its string. "It's over." He turned his upset face toward Martha. "It was fun while it lasted."

Martha loved it when Adam was winning. She needed him to be successful. He was her ambition. She decided that this was not the end of this case and started carefully promoting her new idea.

"Maybe you can investigate more, no? On your own?" She looked at him with her face luminous, as if she'd just washed it. With her tone aiming in between a statement and a question, she added, "Robert does not have to know, does he? Perhaps I could help." Martha's face was glowing. Her eyes were fixed on Adam.

He noticed the twinkle unstoppably multiplying in the deep pool of green. He knew that this always meant an exhilarating adventure.

"That will be all," Josef said, dismissing his new butler, the third one in a row since he started living at the manor. The first butler had thought Josef was a lower-class bum, based on his name and foreign accent. He was out of a job before he could turn Josef's bed.

The second one was very polite. He was also very nosy.

This new butler, an older man, came from Scotland with the best references.

He was still there after many weeks.

Josef leaned back in the sumptuous leather armchair. His palm examined the smooth wood of the massive armrest. His palm reminded him of the ancient wooden railing in his Prague palace, the warmth under his palm as he glided quickly down to open the door for Karel … It was difficult not to think of the past. It was impossible to stay in the present and look only forward. He took one more long sip from the crystal glass filled with fine sherry. Then he swiftly pushed his body up from the armchair. With a few large, springy steps, he crossed to the library as if seeking refuge.

There were books from the floor up, almost to the enormous glass cupola holding the library space together, like a big lid of a candy jar. These amassed treasures_this monument to someone's bibliophilia_belonged solely to him now.

On that crucial first day, it was almost night when Josef, shaken, made it back to the manor.

The place was dark and vacant. It was a perfect metaphor for his life. He'd murdered. He'd lost his soul. He could not feel or think. He fell asleep—more fainted, in fact. When he woke up, he walked around the empty rooms, with furniture covered in white linen sheets. His steps creaked on wooden floors and became muffled by vast colorful carpets. He cleaned himself and shaved, opened some closets, dressed in what could have passed for some kind of foreign travel clothes.

In a few days' time, he calmed down sufficiently to pay a visit to the solicitor.

All went exactly as was suggested in Knud's letter. The solicitor, a man in his late sixties, did not show even a shadow of suspicion. Josef could have relaxed and started living; he had his manor, his money, his bright comfortable future.

If only his lost feelings didn't return. His guilt had formed into a hideous kaleidoscope. Its enormity grew hour by hour until there was no place to turn. Like a toy from those large wooden mechanical German nativity scenes, he walked through the main house, looking straight ahead. He found a vast, well-stocked wine cellar. He knew immediately that this was his way out.

He drank for days and nights. He did not see any reason to hire any staff.

It would not be too long now. Sleepless nights were trading places with confused, sleepy days. He was drinking himself numb to forget and to exit as quickly as possible. But days turned to weeks. Death was not in a hurry to visit him here.

It was a night like any other that week … or was it still afternoon? He'd been drinking continuously since he'd woken that morning. He'd been living on the first floor all that time and kept moving from one room to another with the bottles of wine and sherry. By this day, he'd reached the spacious study. He sat down behind the desk. It was part of a very fine piece of a secretary, with gilded brass details on the top and on all of its drawers. He placed his small revolver on the desk in front of him.

Josef was so saturated with alcohol that he could not get up from his chair. He kept sitting with both elbows on the desk. With the revolver in a sweaty, shaking hand, his world started spinning. He tried to fit his forehead in front of the small killing mechanism. When he thought he had it right, he pulled the trigger. The deafening explosion was the starter's shot of the quick sequence of mishaps that changed Josef's life forever.

When he pulled the trigger, the small revolver kicked back. It happened with much more power than Josef had expected. The alignment of its barrel and Josef's head shifted. The one and only bullet Josef put in burst out, drew a significant curve, and hit the beautifully inlaid secretary. The shot threw Josef's drunken body off balance. He fell and hit the wooden floor. He was trying to sit up when he heard a strange noise from the inside of the furniture. The front of the desk suddenly exploded forward and fell on Josef, leaving him in more pain. Once there was quiet again, Josef looked at the damaged secretary.

The well-calculated, masterfully designed illusion of the fragile piece of furniture was, in fact, a very sturdy safe.

It contained more surprises than Josef could comprehend at that moment.

It was only the next afternoon, once he'd sobered up, that he realized that the Fates had dealt him another hand. He was here to finish a less fortunate, unknown man's work—and not to budge until he completed it. Josef gratefully picked up the tossed glove.

Over the next many days, he discovered this other world of long-abandoned microscopes and innumerable scientific instruments he had never seen before.

There were ancient tools for exact measuring, dissecting, pulverizing. Tools to which he could not attach any purpose at all. Here rested the unfinished oeuvre of an enlightened nobleman who was looking for answers in nature, whose life was cut short some seventy years or so ago. Everything that this unknown scientist strived for lay abandoned under layers of dust made of dried moths and centuries-old pollen. Silklike sticky cobwebs became sheer curtains on large windows in this magnificent space.

Josef didn't hesitate for a second. He was grateful. He accepted, wholeheartedly. He moved in. The world "out there" was not important anymore. Everything, except for his laboratory and gardens, stopped existing. In its own time, his guilt seemed to have subdued. The outer lines of old friends and places seemed to be living behind a screen. Their images were of no importance to "new" Josef, as the long-forgotten scientist in him fully reemerged.

Adam opened the door of his apartment. Rose wasn't home, although it was almost dark. He felt a little touch of panic, immediately replaced by anger that he could be so forgetful. He hit his palm with a fist. "Father!"

He ran quickly to the kitchen and turned on the faucet with cold water. He bent forward and drank straight from it, not minding water rushing out from the corners of his mouth, making his collar wet. The water stream stopped with a loud ringing sound in the brass pipes as he turned off the faucet abruptly. As wet as he was, Adam turned and rushed out the door. His palms ran up his face and over his high forehead as his fingers rubbed cool water into his thick hair. The day had changed into a balmy summer evening by the time he reached his father's house.

"He speaks in tongues. The nurse says it's gotten worse in the last few days." Rose stopped whispering and closed the door behind them. "You are very late," she added in a small voice.

Only now Adam turned toward her and kissed her briefly on her porcelain cheek. "I was very busy."

She put her arms around his long upper arm, almost hanging on him as she was used to doing since she was a little girl.

"Rose!" He shook her off with impatience. In the early years, she would start sobbing, but now she was a well-trained "ballet horse," used to the rough discipline of ballet class and the unforgiving ballet master down in the Old Vic. Small nasty bits like this one couldn't throw her off any longer.

The nurse met with them in the dark hallway.

"I'm sorry, but the new nurse is late. I really have to go now."

"That's fine, Mrs. Dunham. We will stay as long as needed," said Rose, without looking back at her husband. Adam mumbled something that both women took as a sign of agreement. The nurse left, and Adam and Rose stepped into the large bedroom. Father was asleep. Adam always had loved this space. He had been born here and had slept here until he was almost seven.

Tall broad windows overlooked the river. The port was busy—trains waiting for downloads of lumber from boats before heavily chugging away; tall cranes that never went to sleep; sailors; lumberjacks. He was never tired of that vista. It just occurred to him that he'd never thought of photographing it. He picked up his camera hanging around his neck and shot a few pictures from the window.

"Shhh!" Rose looked at him, her index finger across her lips. "Don't wake him."

Adam shook his head and pointed the lens at Rose. Behind her was the photograph of his mother as a young nurse.

She'd died in this room with curtains opened and clean window panes glistening like pools of spring water. The day had been sunny and bright, filled with the giggles of a child from the next-door balcony. Until that moment, Adam had thought that tragedies happened only under gray, overcast skies.

Now, here was the man who had given him life. Almost motionless, in the same bed, fading away before Adam had time to ask him about life. What was Father like as a young man? As a boy? Where was he? Who were his parents? What was his life like before the First World War that altered him for the rest of his life? Adam would never know. His father's injuries had changed his looks. They apparently also had changed his mind. All photographs started at Harewood House, where he'd been sent to heal. He'd met his young wife there.

An elementary teacher, fresh from school, she'd trained as a nurse when the Great War started. For her, it was love at first sight. Father had several medals for acts of bravery. When Mother described them to Adam, they seemed first like heroic actions. As Adam grew older and started judging the world on his own, his father's charges toward the enemy on the battlefields of World War I seemed to Adam more like an attempted suicide.

There was another thing that always had bothered Adam. His father was very talented in singing. His voice had a deep resonance worthy of performance on a radio program. Yet he spent his life running a small pub. After his wife died of pneumonia in the first year of the Second War, he locked himself away from life.

"They were all servants" was his reply to Adam's questions about his youth, his family.

"Father, don't tease! Were they German, or French, or Irish, or Dutch? Or what?" Young Adam's demands were followed by Father's chuckle and the boy's inevitable angry retreat.

"Europe, dear lad, Europe! A little bit of everything! There is Celt in all of us!" His father's amused voice carried behind Adam, the boy with eyes full of burning tears, as he ran away through this very apartment.

All he needed was one good answer … just like now.

Josef's fist wiped his itchy eye, tired after long minutes of focusing on a dissected plant under his microscope. He crossed to the study, poured himself another glass of fine Burgundy, lit up his cigar, and kicked off his shoes. He felt the deep satisfaction of someone who's been helping a friend. Every session in the lab felt like that. His nose inhaled the scent of old leather and polished wood. Home. Stretching his back like a cat, he sank deeper in his armchair and dozed off.

The first thought he had after cold woke him was that of Karel. The wave of guilt was overwhelming. He tried to escape it by falling back to sleep, but that didn't happen. Instead, he started thinking back to the day they met in Prague in the late 1880s…

…Josef followed Baron von Silber backstage at the National. The hallway leading to the male cast's dressing rooms was very narrow and wound around the stage cavern in an unpredictable meander. The smell of new paint was mixed with the stench of wet stones, cheap makeup, resin, glue, and burned hair.

"Your Danish Highness! I brought yet another of the humble subjects of your art!" Baron von Silber's voice was never timid, something Josef never got used to.

The young man was still in his Hamlet costume that gave out a strong odor of sweat and dusty old velvet as he turned towards the visitors. His makeup almost smudged away by the pork grease from the large white porcelain jar, he wiped his right hand into the piece of hemp cloth serving as a towel. Deep brown, almost black eyes with a jolly twinkle looked straight at Josef's pale blue. "Hamlet. At your service."

Josef didn't skip a beat. "Yorick, at yours, Your Royal Highness," and he gestured with a small bow. Both young men burst into laughter.

"You know your Shakespeare, no doubt!" Karel praised the new friend's knowledge of Hamlet's jester and shook his hand. Josef glanced over his shoulder with badly concealed pride at Baron von Silber, who said with a slightly condescending tone, "Given that he saw you at least ten times last season, I am not surprised."

"Karel." The rising star of the National Theater, nodded simply still clutching Josef's hand. Then, in a warm, friendly manner, he added his other hand on Josef's wrist and full-heartedly shook his hands.

"Josef," said the young aristocrat warmly. There was an offer of friendship in the way his words reached Karel.

The baron smiled. Before the tide of the moment could change his plans, he was quickly off toward the hallway leading to the ladies' dressing rooms.

There, he made one last turn, sending a quick salute to the young men.

"You will join us at U Pinkasu, right." Karel turned to Josef, and it was not a question.

The evening had taken the exciting direction that Josef couldn't have hoped for when he'd entered the baron's coach a few hours earlier.

They arrived at the pub U Pinkasu in the middle of a loud debate.

They heard it booming in one of the adjacent rooms. Karel picked up his jug and, shoulder on shoulder, pushed Josef into the smaller noisy room. He chose the table by the door. Someone closed it loudly behind them. The atmosphere of the room changed.

Josef looked up. All faces turned toward Karel and the newcomer he brought with him. "And this is…?"

Josef's upbringing didn't allow him to disguise his identity. Besides, his family name was the guarantee of the old-time honor anywhere in the Bohemian kingdom. He stood up and said his full noble name and his family many predicates out loud.

Karel's hand heavily landed on the wooden table and the foam from his beer spilled around. "All that?"

A few men immediately jumped to their feet with unconcealed enthusiasm. Some raised their jugs, full of the best beer in Prague, in the toast of the centuries-old famous event.

"Everlasting honor to the lords executed after the White Mountain battle!"

Glasses and jugs raised up, they all started calling one over another.

"Honor!"

"Freedom!"

"Equality!"

"Free Bohemia!"

"To brotherhood!"

The level of their sincere devotion was contagious. Josef turned to all sides, his glass high above him in the smoky, almost yellow air. His face luminous, he drank the full jug in one gulp. Everybody cheered as he wiped the foam caught on his mustache with his forearm. Karel looked at him, his dark eyes narrowed into a grin, and nodded in silent accord. Then he said out loud, "Let's go now. They will speak their ideas. You'll get bored." Not waiting for Josef's opinion, he added under his breath, "Plus, I want to hear more about your plans for the future and maybe we will find some fun girls before the night gets too old."

Josef decided to give in. They stood up, arms around each other's shoulders. Josef tossed some coins on the table.

Karel swept them into his palm and spilled them back into Josef's pocket. "My treat tonight!"

Adam heard the phone before he opened the door. The ringing made the studio feel emptier than usual at this time of day. He hoped it was his editor.

He dropped all he had from his hands and grabbed the receiver. "Hello?" He sat down. "When did she die? Yes. I'll be there at once."

His face looked as if he'd moved into another sphere. It remained surprised and shocked until he reached the law firm in central London.

It was a cold late-April day. It was drizzling now, but earlier in the morning he'd noticed frost on the roof across the street. He realized that he had not told Rose to wear her heavy coat. Nobody seemed to mind the weather. It was as if everybody's face carried the good news. Nine years after the end of the war, the rationing was over. He promised to take Rose shopping.

From the very beginning, Josef worked to the brink of exhaustion every day. He cleaned up, dusted, and organized the space until it came back from its slumber. By the time he hired the rest of the staff, the laboratory and his work there were already naturally embedded in the passage of his days.

Here it was where his days started; here it was where they ended. The hours in the days sometimes overlapped as Josef got lost in the big stream of discoveries and his journals. The greenhouse was connected to what he learned was the potage garden—the fresh supply of herbs for the kitchen. It opened further just a few steps down into a lovely sunken Tudor garden with a vast collection of plants arranged into patterns. They were here in abundance, climbing on arches, spreading on low stone walls, existing as miniatures under his feet. All were overgrown and old. Ancient stone walls were in ruins. But altogether, it was a visibly precise, charming design.

Josef was never a gardener. He hired an experienced man. Soon, when he looked out the window, he could see the well-founded garden coming back to life. There were flowers of different species that he could pick up now and study.

His reputation as a strange kind of fellow stopped being news in this part of England. Josef paid taxes and supported local charities and the church, without ever stepping inside. He would pour the vicar a very fine brandy in the living room now and then and generously listen to his reminiscing on his youth in the seminary. Josef's greenhouse started supplying flowers for Easter and Christmas church decoration. Josef made sure, however, that the flowers submitted to the flower show competition were always of the second quality. He did not want to risk winning.

Eventually, all the gossip moved from Josef to something more important, like what the Duchess of Kent wore that week.

To the great chagrin of his fine gardener, Josef never went up the hill to see the newly pruned maze.

Adam found the office without any problem, signed the paper that the solicitor handed to him, and, with the letter in his hand, looked for the closest café. He ordered Viennese coffee and sat down by the window.

The envelope was made of thick double-layered paper. His still-cold, stiff fingers impatiently tore its side. A small key dropped on the tabletop. He enclosed it in his fist and started reading.

Dear Mr. Brandt,

If you are reading this, I am not among the living. I hope I am with Max. He was the love of my life. I didn't want anybody to take even the tiniest bit of him from me; I couldn't bear sharing him.

I was dishonest with you, but I know that you will forgive me now.

Max was an avid photographer. His hobby started being more than that! We had high hopes. He would dress in his shooting jacket and go out for days with his little camera. He finally decided that he was good enough and started collecting photographs in the hope of publishing. The book he planned already had a title—A Photographic Journey Through the English Countryside.

He did not wish anybody to know until he finished the last photo of his work.

It was never finished. As you know, he was taken from me too soon.

I did not report the stolen camera. I couldn't bear that somebody would enter the space in which he was still present for me. I never told my family. Nobody knows this. This key, which I will enclose here, is the key from Max's studio. You will find it at …

Adam finished reading the letter that ended with best wishes to him, personal and professional. Her signature was finished with a curled arabesque left by the swift pen.

Adam was moved. He cleared his throat and wiped tears from his cheeks. He opened his palm. The small brass key was warm from the tight embrace.

He must call Martha and then Robert. He would tell Rose.

Adam sipped absentmindedly from his half-cold coffee. He reread the letter three more times. He ordered another coffee and sipped it hot, almost burning his lips.

No, he would not call Robert. The case was closed. He thought of Max and his wife; they would have wanted it that way. He rang Martha, but she was neither at home nor at her store. Rose, then. Then he changed his mind.

He paid, and waved down a cab right in front of the café.

The windows were cracked open to catch some fresh air. Rose woke up with a shiver. She realized that she'd dozed off. Her point shoe still needed one ribbon. She moved it into the sewing basket for now. She stood up abruptly and felt pain in her bandaged toes and hurt knee. Rehearsals were going well. Her exciting new role was worth all the sacrifice. She paused, uncertain if she was hungry enough to bother with making herself some dinner. Then she decided on a simple sandwich. While fixing it, Rose remembered the book she'd chosen last week from the bookshelf at Adam's father's apartment. She put her miniature dinner on her favorite plate in the colors of alpine lakes and, with a cup of tea in her other hand, looked for the book. Balancing the small load, the book under her armpit, she limped back to the living room and started making herself comfortable on the sofa. She reached for the cushion, forgetting the book. It fell to the floor and broke open. The inner paper connecting the cover-board with the pages was torn. Rose slid onto the floor and carefully picked up the book. Underneath the lining paper, in a secret space, several documents were hidden. Rose pushed them carefully back and closed the book. She crossed the room, hopping on one foot, and turned on the radio.

Adam unlocked the door of Max's studio. It opened to the space so familiar that it made him smile. This was the space of a photography lover. Besides his own work, Max collected and displayed works of many others here. All formats, all genres. Adam was standing in the middle of the time that had frozen over fifty years ago. With professional curiosity and respect, he walked slowly from one photograph to another.

They were everywhere. Hanging on walls, carefully attached inside albums that were piled up on tables, and on the floor. Adam held them up and carefully examined the work. "Bravo, Max!" he finally said into space.

He entered the darkroom. Still pinned to the clotheslines, drying here for half a century, were pictures from the countryside. Some had twisted and curled, but they all looked familiar to Adam. He took them down and brought them all to the large space. Then he sat down in the upholstered armchair. It squeaked, and Adam started coughing. Dust was everywhere. He knew now what he had to do.

But first, he called Rose.

Rose was startled by the phone's ring. For long minutes now, she'd been trying to figure out what to do, what to say, when Adam came home that night.

She was sitting on the carpet, documents from the book spread in front of her. Old sepia-tinted photographs of different people. A handsome dark-haired young man at a costume party, standing very upright with a handsome lady.

Again, a different costume party, it seemed, the same young man in an elaborate Renaissance costume. Then this young man dressed in everyday clothes, hugging another young man.

Both elegantly dressed, captured in a brotherly embrace. The other young man was handsome in a very different way. His face resembled the frescoes she'd seen in one of Adam's art books. The descriptions were all in German and another language unknown to Rose, but it was easy to read the names on the back of the photo: Karel Bernini, Adele Bernini—Prague, 1887.

On the phone, Adam sounded excited on a level Rose had never heard before. It occurred to her that this was not the time to tell him anything. He was not coming home tonight. That was a first.

Her heart sank, but she knew from her ballet master that she was a very good actress. With cheer and understanding, she said, "All right, Adam. Of course! Yes, I do understand. You have to do that. Go. No … don't worry … I'll be fine. Yes. Yes, I have a rehearsal tomorrow afternoon."

Adam followed his excited spiel with "take care of yourself" and "I love you. See you soon." His words suddenly seemed like tedious choreography. Rose did not wish to answer her own bitter question. Her suspicion had been creeping into her mind, bit by bit, year after year. It had grown up with her. The point was that her role of the little girl, the insignificant ballerina, the chorus girl was about to change. She had been working hard on her theater career. She was successful. Now, she also was determined to let that shift happen off stage as well.

She gathered the photographs and laid them facedown on top of the book.

She showered and powdered her body. The clouds of fine microscopic dust sat on everything around her, and for the next few hours the apartment smelled of roses. She carefully painted her lips and made fine black lines above her eyelashes. She brushed the black tint through them as the final touch of her makeup. "Perfect!" She gave herself the highest mark as she looked in the mirror. She carefully pulled on silk stockings and slid into her new form fitting dress.

She waited until her nerves calmed down and then picked up the phone.

She gave the operator a certain number. It had been in Adam's telephone book for as long as she could remember. There was no name attached to it. She didn't know the strength of her jealousy until she found a long red hair wound several times around Adam's shirt button.

Rose sat on the table and crossed her well-proportioned legs, those of a professional ballerina, above her knees.

A young woman answered the phone. Although Rose didn't know, the woman's freckled face always looked freshly washed. The operator said in her indifferent voice, "You may talk now."

Martha felt the rush of excitement from the depths of her body. Adam!

Her eyes darkened one shade of green. "Hello?"

"May I speak to Adam, please?"

Tiny needles pricked Martha's palms. Her armpits were sweating and started to ruin her new dress. "He is not here," she said, and then quickly added, "Who is calling?"

"This is Rose Brandt ... Mrs. Adam Brandt." Then the click concluded this brief exercise in self-control.

Martha was still standing there with the receiver in her hand when the operator asked, "Are you talking?"

Rose felt tangible satisfaction. Her mind was swept clean as if she had been given laughing gas.

She smiled broadly; it was the smile she thought she had forgotten forever during the war. She felt victorious and pleasantly tired. She sat down in front of her mirror. Humming a cheerful tune from her new ballet, she smeared cold cream all over her face.

Martha hung up. There, she thought. It is happening. She'd taken everything she had with Adam for granted. In her book, his name was in every chapter. Martha's mind was as uncontrollable as a whirlwind. If Adam did not care that Rose knew about Martha, then there must be a new woman in his life. A woman who was well hidden from Rose—and from her. Martha didn't see any other explanation. She was not willing to look for one.

She poured herself another glass of red.

"The last time," she promised herself; then she picked up the phone again to call Adam.

Adam did not answer.

She'd always been successful in suppressing jealousy—when there was only Rose, that is. That comfortable arrangement seemed to be over now.

Martha bent her body forward, her face red and temples pounding. She vigorously brushed her red curls. One of them got caught between her lips.

She spat it out with anger. Then she crossed to the window and lit herself a new cigarette.

The new century was just fourteen years young when Crown Prince Ferdinand Habsburg was assassinated by Gavrilo Princip, an anarchist, in Sarajevo.

It was at the end of that hot summer. The war, which had been brewing in the background for quite some time now, broke in Europe.

Two men looked up from their work almost simultaneously.

For years, even when he had the most exciting discoveries under his microscope, Josef couldn't enjoy his everyday life.

The feeling of guilt penetrated all he owned, all he did, all he thought. His nightmare was the reoccurring scene of Max running in front of him and then stopping and taking Josef's picture. Next was the warm jacket against Josef's body, sticking to him as he grabbed Max and stabbed him. Then they fell. Lately, they kept falling into the dusty road more and more often. Josef knew that he shouldn't have read the newspaper all those years back. He was fine until the body he stabbed had a name. "The Theft Murder in Dorset" was the headline. His headline. He closed the library and locked his laboratory. He put all papers with the results of his precision science work in the safe. He visited his solicitor, depositing a few letters that would be opened in case of his death. Reverend gave him a heartfelt hug and blessing that Josef did not resist this time. He heard his cook sniffle; his valet's voice was low with tears. Josef's wish was to fight in the first front. It was granted to him with a firm handshake.

Karel, unlike Josef, had no one to whom to say good-bye. He packed all of his possessions in one medium-sized sailor's sack.

Mary-Ann, the girl he'd met a month after arriving in New York from Philadelphia, went further west a long while ago. He'd watched her leave and felt nothing. Once in New York, he suppressed all he was. His anarchism felt like a story that belonged to another world. His acting was an enchanting fairy tale that haunted him from bottomless glasses of alcohol.

Years ago, he'd started writing his diary in Czech, his secret language.

He created a safe realm to retreat to. Every day he wrote about his childhood, his mother, travels, anarchism, theater, art, his roles. He wrote about his struggle creating characters for plays he was cast in. Shakespeare, Molière, Ibsen, Chekhov, and those he secretly hoped for.

He worked long hours in a shop and started saving money. Then one evening, as he was passing a theater on Broadway, he walked in. Later that night, he drank like never before.

He didn't go to work in the morning. By the time the war broke in Europe, Karel was a pitiful alcoholic. More of a suggestion than the real man in his early forties. His bank account was thin, and his ambition even thinner. He drank and he wrote. Then he heard the newsboys on the street. As if they were grocers selling cabbage, yelling at the top of their lungs.

Without any emotion, their voices drilled into his brain. "War in Europe!"

Karel sobered up. This was his chance. This was his war. Karel did not tell anybody. He packed in secrecy. The boat was leaving early in the morning the next day.

He was an actor who desperately needed a new role. Karel, the knight, put on his imaginary armor and mixed within the legendary knights of King Wenceslas, patron saint of Bohemia. Upon his arrival in London, he was drafted immediately. His archenemy, the Kaiser, and his officers were on the battlefield. He needed to see them. He needed to kill them. It was his romanticism, not anarchism, that sent him to fight at the first front.

Big Ben was announcing noon. The regiment of pigeons noisily left their roof. Adam looked up. He was back in London from his exciting trip to the countryside. He'd already met with an editor friend of his, earlier today. Now he walked through the streets of London, radiating energy.

He called Martha. She was probably shopping in the morning. He would see her later. His walk became almost a jog. He felt great. Things were moving in a new direction. Oncoming waves of excitement were too much to handle alone. He had to talk to a friend.

Adam realized that the Old Vic was close by. Rose had a rehearsal. This will be a great surprise, he thought. He could not remember why he didn't do this more often. He felt the sudden need to talk to Rose. He wished to sit her on his knees again and tell her all the news.

Adam walked through the Old Vic theater stage door and asked for his wife, Rose Brandt. He had to wait. It felt like an eternity. His impatience lifted him from the wooden bench. He mixed, unseen, into a noisy group of dancers.

The hallway that led him toward music and a very loud, impatient male voice held a mix of bitter smells—resin, sweat, and damp shower curtains. He peeked through the glass in the studio door.

Rose was rehearsing with her partner. The feared ballet master explained something to her, and then he turned to a petite lady with gray hair. She stepped toward the rehearsing couple. In her high heels and tight woolen skirt with a slit, she demonstrated. Thickly powdered pale face, black eyebrows painted high on her forehead, hair tightly swept back in a chignon, she opened her delicate, slim long arms.

The movement enchanted Adam, the photographer. He watched, entranced.

The old prima ballerina was showing Rose how to step into her partner's arms without losing her balance or her expression.

The pianist started playing the same part again.

Rose opened her arms. Adam stopped breathing. Her movement enchanted Adam, the man. He had never seen her from that angle. Her subtle silhouette stepped forward with a delicacy he could recall only in old Japanese prints. Her head was slightly bent, expressing her character's doubts; her face, now luminous, filled with anticipation of her lover's embrace. Rose suddenly turned and widely opened her long, slender arms. Her expression changed.

Adam watched, mesmerized. Her small full breasts moving firmly under her transparent chiffon, her shoulders bare, her naked long neck the exclamation mark of her powerful sexuality. With a radiant smile full of love and ecstasy, she stepped into the passionate embrace.

Adam pushed the door open. Master's stick hit the floor.

Rose, still in her partner's arms, looked up, annoyed, and shocked.

Adam rushed from the Old Vic, jealous, angry, and disappointed. Not only could he not speak to his wife, but it was mostly she who did not want to talk to him! He was still in a rage when he entered Martha's little store. The doorbell above him almost fell down as he abruptly opened the door. With his first step, he ran into a large wooden propeller placed by the door. He caught it before it could smash to the floor. He cursed out loud.

Martha appeared from the back of the store. Her fresh face looked as if she'd just washed it. She saw Adam's furious expression and felt a strong urge to giggle.

He pointed his chin at the propeller. "What an idiotic spot for it!" Still, he had to admit, "It's beautiful." He turned and reached forward, running his palm on the smooth wood. "Like silk."

Martha kept standing in the same spot. Her eyes were mellow with an inner smile that she'd felt from the moment she saw Adam.

There was a sadness in it that he could not detect. She did not feel like moving closer. She did not feel like asking him any questions.

"How much?" Adam knew that he had to have the propeller for his studio.

"Oh no, this is not for sale," Martha said quickly.

Adam picked up the challenge, automatically and without enthusiasm. Their foreplay was on again. He didn't feel the usual rush. Did Martha notice? He tried to conceal it. "Well … If I cannot buy it, maybe I can trade it for…" he said playfully.

It came out just a notch too loud. He started making his way toward Martha.

But she kept standing in the same spot, observing him as if he were a street performer. When his arms caught her tiny waist, she said without the slightest hint of flirting, " One young photographer bought it and asked me to store it here for a few hours. He is in the park on the hill. Taking pictures."

Adam stopped holding her. He dropped his arms. What a strange afternoon this turned out to be. Martha watched in disbelief as the door that was never able to close properly slammed behind Adam, sending the doorbell into a frenzy. She made a few slow steps to the closest chaise-longue. She did not sit down.

Josef paid taxes and supported local charities and the church. He established himself as the strange neighbor who sometimes looked mad but in fact, proved to be just a bit of a confused scientist. His manor received a local nickname—the Knud's Place. To his surprise and against his plans, he returned from the Great War, with medals for bravery but unscathed. He submerged himself back in his laboratory work. The seclusion of his English life changed his comprehension of the world. So much so that he forgot all about his political ambitions. He'd stopped listening to the wireless years ago. He was not interested in the newspaper either. He missed the beginning of dangerous political development in the world. When Britain joined the Allies, he was sincerely surprised.

All three men of his staff were drafted. Even in his old age now, his upbringing commanded him to join in the war effort, even in some small way.

For the first time, he felt as if he finally had become one with the village. Later that month, several trucks brought volunteers from the far west shore. They were an odd collection of unaccounted older men, unable to serve any longer, just like Josef. They came to help in the fields.

A few days after their arrival, one of the older men appeared at the manor. Josef carefully opened the door. "What can I do for you?"

"I came to see Knud."

Josef's hand squeezed the doorknob. The other found the knife in his pocket and stayed there.

"Knud? You know him?"

They were standing in the opened doorway. A draft coming from the back rooms was lifting Josef's laboratory overcoat. He felt the breeze running through his hair, pushing it above his eyebrows in a gray cascade.

The man was talkative. "We met in a London pub down by the river in the port before the First War. He was buying ... said he had a castle. We all had a good laugh about it."

Josef waited. "Yes?"

"Imagine my surprise yesterday when somebody said that you have a manor here, called Knud's Place! I thought I had to see it ..."

Josef's senses worked on the full gear again for the first time in a long time. "So now you see it," he said hesitantly, gaining some time to think.

"They said Knud is here. Can I say hello to him?"

Josef shut the door. "Sure." His boots made a crunching sound on the fine gravel.

"What a nice park!" The visitor stood there, looking around. "I see a folly over there." He gave a short whistle through his sporadic teeth. "Has he a maze here, too?"

Josef observed that his own voice was calm. "Yes, he has. In fact, that is where we will find Knud." It all felt as if he was only an observer, passing through this afternoon.

"This is some park!" the stranger said with a slow exhale.

"Just your typical English park, I think," added Josef. "Shall we?"

"Lucky bastard!" said the man under his breath.

In the coming weeks, Josef helped in the village every day, as before. He did not want to be alone. It was a workload that some half his age would have turned down. His anxiety became diluted over time, and he returned to the laboratory and to his writing. The fascicle he was trying to finish was surrounded by notes held by the brown paper tape, with glue on one side. Some days his tongue burned in the evening. More reason to have some fine strong red.

Trucks with volunteers left, and new ones arrived on a regular basis now. An old villager walked up to Josef one day. "I forgot to tell you, Mr. Gunnarsson, there was a man who wanted to see you."

Josef knew this had to come. His shirt already had a sweat stain. He hoped she did not notice the drops that appeared on his forehead. He looked at her, surprised "Really? When?"

"Some time ago. Sorry. I forgot to tell you." Her aging eyes tried to find some spark within.

"Did he say why?"

"He didn't say." She smiled at Josef. He was different. She always liked him.

"No, he never showed up," said Josef, looking at her eyes.

She blushed and looked away. A lock of curled gray hair rolled across her forehead, and she tried to push it under her scarf. "I guess he is gone now."

"I'm sure that he is," said Josef in the most casual way.

Adam was sitting at his studio, waiting for the bell from the darkroom.

His anger was still buzzing in his hairline. As if he stopped being important. To both of them! As if they were in some kind of female conspiracy.

He needed to focus. He crossed and poured himself a glass of water.

During the last few days, he'd taken many pictures, all of them at places he knew from Max's photographs. It was an exhilarating trip. He even allowed himself to go farther afield from his last stop. All that was now developing in the chemical bath.

Through the beauty of mixed woods full of early flowers, he walked along a fast-moving river. He listened to the jolly sounds of bubbling water. Uninterrupted by any other noises, it sounded like the chants of a happy child. It was still early for the bees to be buzzing in meadows and for the blooming crowns of wild fruit trees. The air was cold and clear and carried sounds for miles. Adam heard a train puffing somewhere over the hill.

He got lost first, but then there was a narrow path made, perhaps, by deer or people, which turned out to be a shortcut.

It took him to the midst of mild rolling hills. Soon, he saw an ancient manor with smoke coming from tall chimneys. He kept taking pictures until a voice said, "Good day."

Adam turned. The old man was dressed in a very elegant overcoat, given this was the middle of nowhere.

"A photographer?"

Adam thought he heard a foreign accent in the question. "Yes. Hello."

"How do you do?" The old man suggested a nod.

"How do you do?" Adam's smile was merely a suggestion. He was ready to leave.

"You have a train to catch?" the old man asked.

"Oh no, I stay at the Three Partridges."

"But that is more than four kilometers from here! Youth!" The old gentleman chuckled.

Adam looked up. "A little over three miles … and youth? Thank you … but not for a long time."

The gentleman's smile and the grimace he made covered everything, from his apology for the confusion to his complaint about his old age. Then he pointed toward the manor. "Come, have tea with us."

Adam's shoes were not the best for the country hike. He pictured the blazing fireplace and hot tea. The offer was irresistible.

After V-Day, after the world weaned itself down from frantic celebrations of the victory, Josef thought about locking the house and moving away. At the same time, he knew that the task he was given was not finished. He had to stay. He'd sold a much larger part of the estate this time; more farming land than he had sold when he first arrived before the First War. He was a boy who grew up in two large cities. Countryside, farming, hunting—that all remained foreign to him.

He did not hire any staff for a while. What happened during the war left him with dark dreams. He tried to forgive himself, to reason with himself. "I had no choice," he said to his reflection in the window many times. He stopped looking at his reflections. Josef kept repeating to himself in the following years, "I was given the task. I will make it." His age was slowly changing his daily life. But if he was to finish his work, he also needed to get himself back in shape. He walked back to the gymnasium and tried to lift some weights. They had gained weight over the years, just as he had.

He decided to hire some new help. First, he hired a gardener for seasonal work. Then he read through advertisements for a housekeeper and a butler.

Perkins and his wife were a devoted couple. Perfect for him. They lived for each other and valued their profession. Josef was in the best hands. He returned to the lab, adamant not to lose his focus again.

The bell on the clock rang briefly. It was time to move the photographs from one bath to the next. Adam was already looking at images. Some were really good. What a pity the old man hadn't given him permission to go any farther into the park. He didn't want to be photographed in those superbly furnished spaces of his manor either. Adam respected his wish and didn't prey on his privacy, but he now regretted the lost opportunity. Charming place.

What a lovely afternoon they'd both had! The old butler brought them tea and some sandwiches. They spoke about the previous year's coronation, and about the end of rationing. Adam recalled the old photograph sitting on the side table—two young men in their twenties, holding each other around their shoulders in a warm, brotherly hug. It made a great impression on Adam. All his life he'd yearned to have a sibling. Those two seemed like they had fun together.

Adam had wanted to ask about them, but giving it a second thought, he spared the old man. Here, he had another proof if he needed one. He was not a born reporter.

Another ring interrupted his waiting and stream of thought. He picked up the phone. The operator connected him.

"Martha?"

She didn't say hello to him. Her agitated voice bounced off the walls trapped in the space. This was very unlike her. Adam was not sure how to react. He started explaining.

He had work to finish. His project was very important to him. It was exciting, labor-intensive. Unusual and time-consuming. He needed some time before he would be ready to show it off.

Martha was ironic. He tried small talk. Martha was not in the mood. Her questions were sharply aimed. Adam tried quick maneuvers, like the physical ones from their foreplay.

"No, no!" He tried to protect his work privacy. "Do not come here now! Absolutely not! What...? Nobody's here ... Don't be silly ... What are you talk... No, nothing. Nothing at all ... It's a surprise ... Why don't you believe me?"

He did not have time for this now. He looked at the proofs.

He put the receiver on his thigh. When he heard her pause, he picked up again—this time to lecture her.

"This is unfair, I must say. You should ... Let me ... At least listen ... No! Well, then, I think there is nothing I can say. You must ... Don't be stupid, Martha! Let me explain ... Martha! Martha? Martha! Hello?"

There was a click, and the line stayed silent until the operator asked, "Are you still talking?"

Adam stopped thinking about the conversation the moment his darkroom bell rang again. He thought immediately back to his trip. He thought about what his journey had become. He felt like whistling. It was truly happening. From this afternoon on, it would be the journey of Adam and Max.

He smiled, satisfied. The book of photographs he would publish received its new title: Fifty Years in the Life of the English Countryside.

Rose heard Adam whistling as he came upstairs. She couldn't remember the last time she heard him do that. He couldn't do it, in fact. All he did was blow the air into his lungs. Sometimes she thought he would surely faint when the melody required long notes. She gave a brief, audible giggle, and her closed lips carried on into a smile.

She couldn't wait to show Adam the broken book and help him discover what was hidden there. She decided not to say anything about his rude interruption of her rehearsal.

Adam opened the door, tossed everything he was carrying on the floor, and ran straight to her. Their bodies collided. Rose was not Martha. Rose was … different. Today was different. There was finesse and grace in Rose's movements that he'd never noticed before—not until he watched her rehearse today. The little girl Rose was just an echo from the time past. This was Rose of now. This was Rose, his new lover. They gradually rolled down on the carpet. Adam felt like he was in the middle of an intricately choreographed erotic dance. Rose was no more the girl, waiting for his lead. He gave her his hand and followed.

It was hours later when Adam woke up. Rose covered them with her coat and shawl, but she didn't move away or escape to take her shower, as she used to do. There, in the midst of the smells and scents of their impromptu love, she started telling him about her afternoon with the book.

Adam sat up. "Where is it?"

Rose walked naked into the bedroom. She brought wine and crackers on her way back. Adam lit a few candles. He overlooked the scene where they sat. "Romantic," he said without trying to make fun of it.

Rose handed him his glass and put hers down. She passed him the old photos.

"What made my father collect pictures of these people? I guess I will never know." He looked at the group in historical costumes. A colored postcard of a reproduction of an old painting–it had a handwritten note on its back. Different people, looking very noble. His head, now altered by lovemaking and some burgundy, couldn't make any sense out of it. Over and over, he examined the faces. There was nothing familiar about them. He picked up the postcard again and turned it, looking for the name of the artist. Under the ink of the note, he recognized the printed information. Rembrandt van Rijn:

Family of the actor Giovanni Bernini, Royal Museum, Antwerp, Belgium. Rose handed him the last photograph. Adam did not look at it. Instead, he was still scrutinizing the postcard. He pushed the last photo back to Rose's hand and crossed with unreal brio to his small desk.

He was back with his magnifying glass. Rose was bewildered and excited, seeing him so profoundly happy. He looked again and again, wiped his forehead, and spun around. She had never seen him act as if he was a little boy. "Adam, what is it? Adam?"

He could not talk; he just handed her the magnifier. Rose played with the distance to find the sharpest focus. There. Now she saw it too—the name of master Rembrandt was slashed into two parts by an almost invisible line: Rem/brandt.

Rose turned the postcard. "What does this mean?" She was spellbound by the baroque fashions of the portraits. An enchanting, colorful group of the Italians.

Adam stood there, overwhelmed. "I cannot tell you....but Brandt...Brandt is my surname."

"Ours," she whispered, and he smiled at her.

Rose handed the last photo to Adam without thinking much about its possible significance anymore.

"I know this!" Adam looked as if he was getting ready for a sprint.

Rose took the photo from his hand. Two young men in their twenties, holding each other around their shoulders in a brotherly hug.

"Rose, I saw this one in the manor."

"You have to go back," said Rose, to his surprise.

"I know."

Rose brushed her face towards his chest. "I will be here when you come back."

Adam's mouth led her up, and he said in an almost inaudible voice, "I adore you."

One hour past midnight, Martha picked up her phone again. Her conversation was short. When she hung up, she felt immediately guilty about it.

What if Adam came back unexpectedly? Of course not! She knew by now he would not. That thought just hurt her further. Once he married, their long nights together were over. "Little girl Rosie." The words came out as a surprise as if she was saying "Who would have guessed?" She was angry with Adam all over again. She was angry with herself, with the fact that Rose made her feel jealous. More than any other woman ever will.

A few drinks later, her doorbell rang. Martha gave a last-moment glance to her slender figure in the tall Venetian mirror. It was the contour of her full breasts above her tiny waist that drove Adam crazy. She opened the door.

"Thomas!"

Her face looked as if she had just freshly washed it. Her broad smile with hints of rouge illustrated her decision. Her tongue touched her upper lip. She projected all of her nakedness in that small gesture. The young photographer, whose propeller she'd stored for the afternoon the other day, stepped barefoot onto the long Persian runner.

"Nurse! Helen!"

"Mr. Brandt? Mr. Brandt, wake up!" The new nurse in Carl Brandt's bedroom was trying to bring Adam's father out of his dream. "Here, I will give you another shot. You will feel better quickly."

Before he could say anything, she did it almost as gently as his Helen would have.

"Helen, my tin box … my book … bring it."

"Which book, Mr. Brandt? I'm Claire. Your new nurse." Her voice was gentle, upbeat, trained to avoid conflicts with children and elderly patients. Always mindful not to remind people of their memory lapses. Always more suggesting than asking straight forward.

"Heinrich Mann. Big book. Henry IV. Thick and blue."

The nurse wanted to help. She liked this old man. He resembled the men she knew at the end of the last war. That chapter was over; she didn't wish to slide her finger along that bookmark.

Now, she stood in front of the tremendous bookshelf. It was much larger than any she'd ever seen in ordinary middle-class homes. She noticed the titles in English and some, to her surprise, in German. A blue book. Big.

She found it. Next to Karl Marx's Das Kapital, there was Heinrich Mann's Henry IV. She had to bring a chair from the dining room. She pulled out the book and let Das Kapital fall down on To Have and Have Not. She stepped down and sat back on the chair. Her patient had fallen asleep. She was happy that the noise of falling books did not wake him. She picked them up and placed them back exactly as they were before. This was her perfect opportunity to glance into the book she'd always only heard of. Heinrich Mann's Henry IV was heavy, serious reading about the history of the Huguenots, Henry de Navarre, and Saint Bartholomew's night massacre. She opened the frontispiece—and lost her speech.

She did not know what to do. Then, she picked up the telephone.

Josef lit his cigar and placed it in the ashtray. He hasn't smoked for years now, but he loved the perfume of it. He was waiting. He had been waiting for years for things to happen. For someone to come and close his life into a full circle. Wars had not done it, as he'd hoped. He kept working in the lab, but it was just a habit now. He picked up his cigar, inhaled with delight, and slowly let the smoke out before placing it back in the ashtray.

There was an interesting dilemma he wished to solve. He looked out the window across the rolling hills. How was this possible? He meets a young photographer by pure chance in his fields, and the young man has Karl's mannerisms. Or does he? Josef's mind was confused and amused at the same time but certainly intrigued. Perhaps Josef's senses had played a jest on him. Perhaps he was projecting his deep wish into this accidental meeting. Was it accidental?

The ever-latent spy in him started doubting. Josef had observed the young man carefully as he'd looked at the photograph the other day. All he said was that he wished to have a brother. No, he was not related to Karel; the photograph meant nothing to him. But the way he moved, the way he chuckled, the way he stretched his arm, his "How do you do?"—Josef saw Karel in him and was attracted. He sat down and started weighing the possibility of his finding this photographer in London. He rang the small brass bell placed on his vast desk, and the butler entered the office.

"Perkins, how would you look up a photographer's address in London?" Just like many times before, the man had an immediate idea. He was indispensable.

But before he went away, he tactfully reminded Josef, "Sir, about the next week…"

Josef remembered. "Uh, yes, of course, the funeral of your aunt. Your wife said she would have things ready for me in the refrigerator."

"Very well, sir. Thank you, sir." Perkins bowed his head slightly. It was settled, then. He and his wife, Josef's housekeeper, were going on a trip.

Perkins left without Josef's noticing, as he was already submerged in growing excitement and memories …

Martha promptly sat up to escape the last scene of her dream in which she was climbing too high on a tower. She didn't like that feeling. Dreams. They did not give any answers. But then … maybe she was right. She didn't need any help deciding. She would go away. To America. It was the place she'd always wished to visit. Unlike

Adam, whose father instilled in him the picture of America being noisy, unfriendly, chaotic, and busy, she saw it differently through the pictures in her magazines. Her America was full of sunshine, colorful fashions, and people smiling from one ear to another with perfectly white, symmetrical teeth. She looked at the sleeping body next to her. She heard the first trams from afar, birds trying to wake up the park. Distant calls from boats on the Thames made her feel lonely. She kissed the young man's naked shoulder and pulled the blanket over her head. She spooned her lover's body and rested her face on his naked skin. Thomas stirred. He didn't wake up. Martha turned on her back and closed her eyes.

"Rose?" Adam whispered tenderly. Rose did not hear him. She was still deeply asleep. He tried again with the same gentleness. "Darling! Wake up!"

"Bugger!" Sweet Rose sat up.

Adam fell back in bed, laughing. "The fact that you shagged me through the floor all night, Mrs. Brandt, doesn't mean that your foul mouth will be toler—"

She jumped at him and, while giggling, covered his mouth with her palm, pushing him backward in the pillows.

"Stop, stop, stop!"

"Oh, so it's all right when you say it ..."

Adam locked her head under his upper arm. She fought with the vigor of a ten-year-old. Then she gave up, or did he let her win? She kissed him in his hair, her small full breasts dangerously close to his face. "All right! Peace! I promise never to say it again!" Rose looked at the alarm clock. "Oh no! Darn, darn, da-a-a-rn! I am fucking late!" She ran naked to the bathroom and then off to life, leaving her fresh scent behind.

Spring was ending on a colder note. Adam decided to stop at the studio first and change into the traveling jacket he'd left there. The old man was certainly dressed with the Victorian sense for daily sartorial changes. Amused by the thought, Adam decided to play along. Victorians! The man is really old. Just like his father. Father! Adam forgot to stop at his father's yet again this week. He packed a few things and grabbed his camera. Once on the street, Adam turned up the tweed collar and waved down a taxi.

Nurse Claire answered the door. "Mr. Brandt, I have a few important things I need to talk to you about." Adam looked at her, worried. "There is nothing wrong medically," she said immediately, with professional affirmation, but then just as immediately, she corrected herself. "I mean, there is nothing new, as far as your father's health condition."

"Yes?" Adam leaned against the oak chiffonier in the hallway and asked boldly. "Do we owe you money?"

The nurse blushed and shook her head. "Oh no, no." She continued with a soft voice as if unfolding a bouquet of fragile flowers. "You see, I served in the last war. In the end, I was nursing some soldiers from the Eastern Front. The nurse I replaced, Mrs. … Mrs. …"

"Mrs. Dunham," Adam said helpfully.

"Yes. She told me that your father started speaking in tongues."

"I remember. She said that it got worse." Adam looked at his watch and toward his father's bedroom. "I am sorry, but I would like to—"

"Your father is asleep now." The nurse looked at him apologetically.

Adam relaxed, reclining against furniture again.

"You know, Mr. Brandt, he does not speak in tongues. He speaks in … I think it's Russian. Here…" Adam noticed only now the blue book she was clutching in her folded arms. "This is what he asked me to hand to him."

She placed the heavy print of Heinrich Mann's novel in Adam's hands.

"Henry IV? My father wished to read to himself?"

Nurse Claire lifted the cover page. Adam's mind went blank.

Martha was packed. Her decision came quickly. She acted upon it before she could change her mind. She pulled the shutters down over her antique shop windows. She gave her keys to Thomas. She would be back in a few months.

She wrote a long letter to Adam but didn't post it.

Her taxi was coming soon, her suitcase was sitting where the propeller had been. Her telephone rang. She did not pick up. "I am not here," she instructed herself. She thought for a moment. No, she observed with indifferent sadness, no, she couldn't feel any honest emotion for Adam anymore. "It is as well," she said aloud as if some stranger had died, and she'd decided not to go to his funeral. Venetian looking-glasses on all sides of the old antique store reflected the young woman with the freckled face. Even now, it looked as if she'd just freshly washed it. With her new, elegant beige trench coat over her arm, she looked like a lucky tourist. However, the large dark glasses she'd put on this morning were not a fashion statement.

Adam reached inside the hollowed space in the book. He carefully removed the red sashes that held the thick notebook together and opened it in the middle. Then he sat down on the runner in the hallway. The nurse brought him a chair.

He made her sit down on it while he carefully inspected the finding.

It was a diary. A cutout from an old magazine fluttered like a leaf to the ground. Adam picked it up and put it to the side on the carpet. The black-and-white reproduction didn't catch his eye. Adam speedily flipped through the diary. He was mesmerized.

A name written on top of the page caught his attention. He pulled out the envelope from his pocket, took out the photo of the young man, and compared names. The name sure was Karel Bernini. He looked at it without the slightest idea of what to make out of it. Without thinking, he reached for the cutout to put it back between the pages.

He stopped, and took out the postcard he already had. It was the same Rembrandt. This one without any marks. Adam needed to ask his father a million questions, but the sleeping man next door was beyond the point of reach. Adam's mind stirred thoughts and mixed them with a lifetime of his fantasies.

Who was that man next door? Where did he come from? When? How? Why? Who was he? Who was Adam?

Adam could not stand the pressure of his questions or the dark hallway or the old smells of this apartment any longer.

"I'll hold on to this … I have an appointment. I will come back later!"

His thoughts were already running way ahead of him. He had a train to catch.

This time Adam knew where to get off the train. In front of the picturesque station, he hired a local cab. "Monksfeld Park," said Adam through the rolled-down window. The taxi driver hesitated. Adam sat himself down in the back and put his camera on his knees. "That's what my Baedeker guidebook says." Adam pointed his finger on the map. The driver had no idea where to go. Adam waved his hand. "Back somewhere over there!" Then he added impatiently, "I was there already. In the fields … There's a manor with a large garden and a greenhouse."

The driver woke up and, to avenge himself, said to Adam with the intonation of someone superior talking to an idiot, "Oh, you mean the Knud's Place?" And he shifted into first gear.

—⚭—

Adam stood on perfectly raked fine gravel. The broad driveway was surrounded by a sharply trimmed lawn. The peppery sweet scent of freshly cut grass still lingered in the air, but the gardener had left for the day.

Adam looked up at the ancient building as if seeing it for the first time. It was beautifully proportioned, elegant, and photogenically worn down. He took a few pictures. "Charming!" he said aloud.

He hung the camera back around his neck and rested his hands in the pockets of his tweeds. His fingers tried to calm down. He'd hoped for a little candy.

"My Baedeker!" He'd left his guidebook in the cab. Too late now ... He didn't have time to get upset.

Josef, elegantly dressed, golden pin in his silk cravat, stood there, composed, with open arms. "Welcome back."

"Hello again." Adam smiled, surprised by the welcome. Suddenly a bit shy, he slightly swayed back and forth. "Hello again, Mr. Gunnarsson! Knud Gunnarsson? Right?"

Josef lifted his eyebrows. "The taxi driver?"

Adam nodded. "He told me everything, and all that which he did not know."

They sat down in the library. Josef offered Adam a cigar; then, gently shrugging his shoulders in disbelief that his luxurious offer was turned down, he lit one only for himself. He inhaled very slowly.

Deep, visible pleasure closed his eyes. Without any rush, white clouds of smoke twisted and meandered above the party. No one spoke. For sheer fun, Josef puffed out several times in a short sequence, creating smoke rings. He chased after them in the air and poked them with his fingers. Here was the side of him that enchanted Adam, the little boy.

One more set of smoke rings and then … "I was ready to go and search for you in London. And now, here you are."

Adam was pleased. He was afraid that his enthusiasm and growing affection would scare the old man away. He measured his words, trying to smile as he talked. "You see … I had to come back. There is a picture in the living room … the two young men …" Adam pointed somewhere behind him and did not stop smiling.

"My study now," Josef corrected Adam, but it sounded also like a command. Josef stood up with surprisingly youthful vigor. With the smoking cigar clutched between his teeth, he led the way.

The inlaid polished wooden floors made creaky noises under their quick trots. The place smelled of beeswax and patchouli. Sunshine was flooding the room. It was like entering a transparent piece of amber.

Josef picked up the photograph of the two young men from the fireplace mantel and placed it on the desk. Adam stepped next to him and slowly put his copy beside it as if he was playing an ace in cards.

Josef sat down. He felt dizzy. His heart skipped several beats. So it was true. For the last few days, he'd had time to think and rethink the chance-meeting in the fields. He'd postponed the sale of those acres.

After a pause, he said firmly, "You are Karel's son."

Adam's body moved in two miniature waves, back and forth. He spoke with hesitation, looking at the twin photographs. "Karel Bernini? I think … I am not. My father is Carl Brandt…" Then, almost immediately, he started rephrasing his doubts. "You see, I am not sure of anything anymore. I think that in fact … I do not know who I am." Then he reached into the deep inside pocket and pulled out first the diary and then the old photographs. "Here is why I came back here."

Josef dropped his cigar into the ashtray and reached for the booklet.

He opened the diary. His hands were shaking now; his thighs felt weak as if he just had returned from a long run. There was the old feeling of a void in between them. He stood up and then sat down again, moving in anguish before leafing through the pages. His anxiety made his fingers clumsy and chaotic. Even his signet ring felt unusually heavy and large, restricting his movement. He took it off and placed it on the small tray among fountain pens. He pointed to the glass bar near the wall.

Adam understood and crossed the room. He poured Josef some brandy.

"For you too," suggested the old man. It was already clear to Adam that they both would need more than just that. He walked slowly back with both full glasses and handed one to Josef.

Adam didn't look for a chair; instead, he knelt down on the floor in front of Josef. He did it without thinking, subconsciously, perhaps in an attempt to reverse time, to be a little boy again. He looked up at Josef, his face open and waiting. This was the man with the answers to all of Adam's questions. He took a gulp of brandy and asked, "Who is Karel Bernini? Why did someone divide Rembrandt's name on the postcard? Who were the Berninis?"

Josef shook his head. In silence colored by the fragrant spring breeze blowing in from the park and by bird love calls from all around, he opened the diary almost ceremoniously. He would have kissed the old pages, had he not felt ashamed.

The unknown language started to unravel in front of an amazed Adam. Josef began reading and then slowly translating from the long-lost language of his youth.

"January 1887. I was cast as Hamlet. Adele, my superb mother, was my Gertrude. She is the brightest star of European theater! I observe her with enthusiasm every evening. I love her like no son ever loved his mother! She tells me the secrets of her acting." Josef randomly turned a few pages.

"It is impossible to talk to Father about anything. Such a fine actor! But he doesn't know how he does it. He always fails to explain to me anything about acting. He simply has no idea how it happens for him. Is that why he pushed me to be a lawyer?"

A few more pages forward. "Anarchism is all I need to balance my life with. Theater means everything to me. But there is a deeper purpose in serving the general good. I always knew how to write well. I wrote great pamphlets. All of the Empire thought that I was running the whole thing! I tricked them all!"

A few pages back. Josef slowed down as if the sharp pain in his injured back reemerged. "Sophie-Ann was lying there. Blood all over her head. Josef didn't want us to leave. I had to push him. His aristocratic pride! They would have shot us, had they found us."

Josef paused there, he wanted to comment, but then he changed his mind. He turned more pages and kept reading. "I shouldn't have yelled at him. We parted badly. Did he ever get on the boat? Did he stay in Hamburg? I hope not. Did he cross the Channel? Maybe he is here in America ..."

Pages later. "I never saw him again. I never heard of him. Such talent! He could have been prime minister by now. I looked for him on the battlefields. I knew he must have been fighting on my side ... our side ... if he was there. Did he ever try to look for me? Am I dead for him? Is he ... dead?"

Josef stopped reading and bent forward. His arched back expressed all of his misery. He never looked for Karel. Not ever. He assumed that he perished somewhere in America. The upholstered chair turned into the sandstone step in the old palace in Prague.

"Mr. Gunnarsson?" Adam whispered, trying to be as polite and patient as possible. But he'd come here to find answers to his questions—to all of them.

Josef composed himself. "Yes, of course. I will have a sip ... Let me translate toward the end, I am curious ... here it is, then."

"Is that Russian?"

Josef looked up with a surprised expression. "Russian? No..."

Josef took another sip. Adam did too. Refreshed. Josef continued.

"The young nurse was like an angel to me. She would come every day. Her tender fingers changed my bandages. It never hurt. I was unable to see her, my own Cordelia, but in her voice was everything I ever wanted."

Josef interrupted his reading here and looked at Adam_

"No, this is not Russian. This is Czech." And then, leaving Adam perplexed, he returned to his translating.

"Everybody said it was my beautiful, gentle Helen who healed me. She didn't care about my scars. She agreed to be my wife."

Adam raised up on his knees. "Helen?"

Josef looked up from the diary and nodded. "Yes?"

Adam sat back on his heels and finished his drink. "That was my mother's name. She was a nurse in the Great War." Adam stood up insecurely and picked up the photographs of the hugging young men. "Who is this? Who are they?"

Josef ran a quick flickering film in his head and then decided. "All right, I will tell you, then. This is…" He lost his breath in a gulp of emotions and inhaled again to finish his sentence. He said as quickly as his old voice allowed him. "They were my best friends." He paused and then added with the deep emotion tightening his throat, "The dark one is your father, Karel."

Adam could not process this. He seemed to not understand. His silence made Josef repeat.

"Karel Bernini. And this"—he put his palm on the page— "this is his diary." Josef closed the cover and returned the booklet to dumbfounded Adam. Then he looked again through the other pictures. "All these are photographs of him, his mother, his father." With admiration undiminished by decades, he added proudly. "Karel was a star. The greatest star. Like his mother, Adele … your grandmother."

Adam stood there stunned and then began talking slowly, almost a whisper. "The scars run from his forehead to his jaw. Deep and…" He'd wanted to say "ugly," but now, after all he had heard, it seemed suddenly inappropriate.

Karel … Carl … All his life Adam thought his artistic talents came from his joyous swinging mother. He thought his father uninteresting, backward, unambitious. He always doubted his wild heroism on the battlefield.

Now he understood that his father's greatest heroism was his life without theater.

Josef had to know. "Is he … around?"

Adam waited for a moment. "Yes … no…"

"Pardon?" Josef saw Adam's face turn paler.

"Ever since my mother died, he keeps declining. He doesn't know who he is anymore. He is very weak … sleeps … speaks in tongues … in Czech, I mean … nowadays. Almost entirely. He doesn't recognize us most of the days."

Josef fell deeply into his thoughts. After long minutes, as if coming in from a long walk, tired, exhausted, he said aloud, "Prague was such a magical city … old palaces … gardens … Charles Bridge. The ancient university. The vast, calm river. The National Theater."

"Who was the dead girl?" Adam could not wait any longer.

Josef looked straight in front of him. His voice rasped from his throat. Without any intonation, he said, "Sophie-Ann von Silber, the imperial minister's daughter."

"Why was Karel … my father … with her?"

"He was not. I … his friend was … I mean, yes he was … it was the letter he wrote that…" Josef pointed at himself in the photo.

Adam did not understand. "What letter?"

Josef did not answer. He opened the diary where two pages were glued together. Adam hadn't noticed them until now. Josef reached for the letter opener and split the pages open. Each page had a drawing in black ink on it.

On the left page was a circle with capital A in its center. On the right, the capital A was placed in the middle of a jingle bell.

"Anarchism was such a fascinating idea. We all thought…" Josef's unfinished sentence only opened new dark avenues in Adam's mind. He was familiar with assassinations, bombings, murders. All done in the name of anarchism, in the name of the idea that remained foreign to him. And then, of course, there were horrible punishments. He read about the history of anarchism while in the police force. Many got shot on the run and executed. Adam saw pictures, photographs, and paintings of that gruesome history. But to imagine that his father would be one of those men? He realized that the man here was probably also one of them. A few moments ago, Adam was happy and proud of his father, but now, he was uneasy sitting here. Was his father an assassin? Was he a murderer? He did not dare to ask.

All this time Josef kept observing Adam. Suddenly, he was not certain how to continue this conversation. He was waiting for the big question. Josef's old worn-down senses started forming a doubt. A small drop of suspicion about the reason why this man had come here formed somewhere in Josef's brain. Adam's interest in finding the truth about his father seemed genuine. But one never knew. Helped by the amounts of alcohol they'd already consumed, Josef, whose complicated life was devoid of feeling relaxed, was quick to form a web of suspicion. What if this man already knew everything? Russian? Didn't everyone know that they didn't use the Latin alphabet? How did he find Josef in the first place? A chance meeting in the fields close to the manor? Sure …

Josef looked at Adam. It all started being too strange. The diary was genuine, though. He poured one more round. He had a history of finding excuses for Karel. Now again, for his son? His so-called son …

Adam did not look at Josef as he slowly brought the glass to his lips. He acutely wanted to know everything that this old man could tell him. At the same time, he feared the answers. His mind became fogged by alcohol, his body was relaxed, his coordination blurred. After a long pause, he finally tried to say something, still holding his glass at his lips. He choked and, in a fit of coughing, spilled the sticky ruby-red liquid all over himself and the carpet.

"Bugger! I'm so sorry!" He looked for something to start cleaning the accident.

"There is a water closet back toward the kitchen." Josef pointed to the hallway. "There should be extra towels in there. That's all right. Don't worry about it too much. They will clean it tomorrow."

Adam smiled back at him. He took off his jacket, held it away from his body, and then dropped it from the height of his head onto the floor. Josef knew this ritual. This is what Karel would do. Like a boy, Josef relaxed a bit. His eyes changed their shape as his cheeks lifted up into what was undoubtedly a fatherly smile. Reminded of his never-realized family life, Josef started rethinking this unexpected chance, diluting all his suspicion. Maybe this is all genuine. Maybe this is the moment. He could help. He could not reverse Karel's life, but he could change it for his son. He immediately loved the idea. The strength of his enthusiasm took him by surprise.

That's it! He would call his lawyer in the morning. He would adopt Adam. This whole estate, all of his life's work, his collections, all would have the best of custodians. Josef took a sip from his glass, and it was not just the fine liquid that started warming his body. Josef felt the deep satisfaction of a life coming to a sensible culmination after tragedies, suffering, loss. The purpose of his life was right here. It took a long time, but it finally arrived. He bent to lift the young man's jacket. He smiled and thought of how many times he'd picked up Karel's jacket from his floor; he chuckled.

One more photograph spilled out of the breast pocket. Josef put his spectacles back on and turned the photograph.

Everything that had happened up to this second seemed to be in some other dimension. Everything that he became in the last few minutes left at that one instant.

Josef sat down heavily into his armchair. His eyes were fixed on the image in the photograph from Adam's breast pocket—intricate patterns of black and white pebbles, with a dead man's body lying face down, his shirt soaked with blood around the apparent knife wound. The man was stabbed in his back. Josef's trembling hand turned the photograph face down. The rapidity of his mind concurred with his heartbeat.

Adam felt totally stupid after spilling his drink. Had he stayed any longer in the room, he was certain, he would have started stuttering again.

Kitchen? Did the old man say straight ahead? Adam's drunken mind focused on every step. He tried to go to the end of the hallway. It split into three corridors. What now? He did not want to look incompetent. After all, he was Karel Bernini's son. He smiled. The buzz in his head relaxed his senses.

He felt like giggling. He thought he heard a tap dripping. He was right. There was a kitchen. "Water closet—that's what the old man … friend … had said … wa-ter… clo-set …"

Adam exited the kitchen and got back to the hallway intersection. He must be very drunk after all. The next door was opened to the gymnasium. A solid old-fashioned one with swords, sabers, and rib stalls. All in frequent use, it seemed. That old man sure knew how to live.

Josef tried to think calmly. First, he put the photo where he'd found it and dropped Adam's jacket back on the floor. Then he sat down again. His knees were weak. The hollow feeling in his thighs returned now. He heard Adam somewhere down in the hallway. He wished to stop time.

The diary of his whole life was flickering in his mind like the first cinematograph he'd seen as a little boy in Vienna. He sat motionless, unwilling to move. His emotions were as raw as on the day Sophie was killed, as painful as in that second when he pushed the blade through Max's chest.

Now, he got up and quickly crossed to his laboratory. He tried not to make much noise. His revolver was in the third drawer. He put it in his pocket. Having second thoughts, he turned, took the large volume of his finished research from the desk, and returned to his office.

Adam was back with towels, water, and vinegar. His dizziness from the strong drink didn't go away.

"You are very thorough, my friend." Josef allowed Adam only to start with some cleaning. He stopped him with a jovial, "Enough, enough! I pay people to do that." Josef placed the large thick volume of bound papers in front of Adam. "Look at this—my life's work."

Adam looked at the volume. It was an outstanding collection of scientific drawings. The precision and beautiful handwriting were remarkable. It was a very large volume. He tried to be polite but then looked out of the window. The sun was out, skies high, no clouds.

Josef saw his look, apparently, because he suggested a walk through the park. "You came to photograph, no?"

They stepped out on the terrace that led them down to the low Tudor garden and farther into the park. Adam started taking pictures. Josef kept encouraging him to look around and choose new angles. To Adam's surprise and delight, he even posed for one. No restrictions this time.

They left the garden grounds and stepped into the English park. Tremendous vistas opened unexpectedly before the enchanted photographer.

A rare landscape architecture, the whole park was a gem. Adam was sure he had never heard of it. He thought of Max. He wished he could show all this to him. He took more pictures.

Josef and Adam were approaching what looked like a small temple created entirely from hedges. Adam became excited—a maze in the English park!

They walked heavily up the hill. Josef was already inside the green structure. Adam hesitated. So much to take in! He turned and photographed the folly on the horizon. Then he too entered. The height of the walls turned the light into a green haze. Adam kept looking up the leafy walls and, as planned by the skillful architect a few centuries ago, got lost. He stopped at the lush green dead end. The leaves were interspersed with yews here. Adam started backtracking his own steps. He felt light embarrassment when he called, "Help me! I'm lost!"

Josef heard the words that froze his blood in the decades-old flashback.

Adam tried to find his way out.

"Mr. Gunnarsson?" He retraced his steps and was now at the beginning of the maze. He looked across the park. A small red tractor was crossing the field on the horizon. Maybe he should stay out here.

Josef's voice came from not far ahead. "Keep coming!"

Adam reminded himself that he was here to get answers. He turned and stepped back into the maze.

The outer world became just a muffled soundtrack. Adam moved in a leafy dream. He made yet another turn. Josef was quiet now.

"Mr. Gunnarsson?"

"Turn first right. Keep on right."

Adam looked at the path. The grass gave way to scattered pebbles.

The walls were solely yews here. Now he heard the old man's breathing somewhere close. He made one more turn. One glance under his feet, and he stopped, petrified. The ground changed abruptly into the intricate pattern of black and white pebbles.

Josef stepped out of his hiding place, the old revolver pointing at Adam's face. "So now you know who I am."

Adam was so shocked that he couldn't find any words to respond.

"Enough of this game, please." The revolver pointed at Adam swayed. Josef had to clutch it with both hands. "You found me at last. Well done! Did you come to me for money? To blackmail me? You did not really think that I would agree to that."

Adam just stared at Josef. What happened to the kind old man? How?

He stood there facing the black muzzle of the revolver, and he could not move. His voice faltered as he tried to say something. He feared that his stutter would finish his speech. When he finally spoke, he did it slowly, carefully enunciating. His every word was a monument to his nerves.

"I did not find you. I did not look for you. I d-did not know you were my father's"—he paused and took a deeper breath and then exhaled—"friend."

Josef's face suddenly assumed a new strange look. He suggested a bizarre bow of a jester. His revolver made a dangerous turn. "Yorick. At your service." And then he added, with unexpected sadness punctuating every syllable, "Karel Bernini was the best Hamlet that ever walked this earth..." He shook his head in amused disbelief. "Carl Brandt. Genial! How typically Karel ..."

On hearing his father's names, Adam saw his chance. "You were the one who noticed. It was you who told me." Adam tried to defend his reasons why he'd come here.

But Josef, clutching the revolver with both hands, made a step forward. "You are the one who spied around! So now you know it all ... and you know where we are, right?"

Adam's eyes refocused from the revolver back on Josef's face.

Josef's old eyes narrowed. They looked more slanted than ever before. "The photograph in your breast pocket ... how do you explain that?"

Adam opened his mouth. He made no sound. His trembling fingers touched his jacket. Only now did he realize that he'd changed at his studio that morning. It was only to please Josef, to play the Victorian game. It was too late now for any explanation. He would pay for his servility.

The old man holding him at point-blank range knew his own truth. He was in no mood to hear anybody's reason or to back up now.

"Yes, I killed him. I killed the bastard who tried to cut my throat..." Josef had to take a breath before he could continue. "And whose name I had to assume!"

"Name? Whose name?" This all was far larger than Adam could fathom.

"Then ... the man ... the poor man ... he called for help!" Josef shouted as if in desperation and paused, breathing loudly. His voice changed to a whisper. "I had to kill him ... I had to. I had no choice. I had to murder ... him ... poor Max..."

Adam's face looked like a personified scream. He stood there, now completely sobered up. The blurred photograph, the shadow of a figure flashed inside his eyes. "Max?"

Josef's voice gained resonance again. He pronounced every word as if chewing on something disgusting. "You see? All this ... all this ... killings ... murders ... all for one spoiled, capricious, jealous girl!" He was running his words sharply through his accumulated sorrow and bitterness. "There was no way back. We had no way back ... Can you imagine? No forgiveness. No one to talk to. All of our lives ... gone ... smashed ... erased ... All for one caprice—" He paused, and then suddenly his voice regained the bright tone of his youth. Full of enchantment, he exhaled on one breath. "She looked ravishing that night." There, his voice imploded, and they stood in deadly silence.

Then, softly again, from the deepest layers of his suffering, Josef's voice came back. "You see now ... now I have to do this. You understand ... I have to do this?" Josef took a deep breath and clutched his revolver tightly. His knuckles turned pale and translucent. His voice moved into low tones. He put weight on every word. His diction was ice; the meter of his speech was punishment. "I, Josef Maria Leopold Johan von Kaplitz, knight of the Saint Constantin Order of Chivalry, Count von Chastolar of the most noble family of the Bohemian kingdom, I confess that I am guilty of murdering innocent men!"

As he spoke, his voice roughened with tears he tried to swallow.

He did not stop looking at Adam. He did not stop pointing at him. Only now he lowered his revolver and aimed at Adam's chest. His teeth clenched; he was more spitting than speaking.

"I am so sorry. I am so very sorry ... but I have to do this. Forgive me if you can ... Forgive me ..."

Adam closed his eyes. He had no thought in his head. No prayer. No regret.

A deafening sound shattered his sense of pain as he collapsed. His knees painfully hit the black and white pebbles. His blood started seeping through the fabric.

Josef's body fell to the side. A thin stream of blood ran from his temple, where he'd placed the killing shot.

Adam, numb to his torment, knelt there staring at his father's dead friend ... his friend. Then he curled up on the black and white pebbles; his body started shaking beyond his control. Long minutes passed. Adam finally managed to stand up on his weak legs. Stumbling, he slowly crossed the small space and, ignoring pain, dropped back down on his bleeding knees.

He put his arms around Josef's dead body and wept.

EPILOGUE

Adam sat in Josef's study, a half-full glass of sherry in his hand.

He made a few more telephone calls. Police had just left. Arrangements were made. Rose was waiting for him at home. The day had stayed bright, like a day in which only happy events are allowed. Adam walked to the window. He forgot to think about Martha.

The small red tractor on the far hill was still crossing the dark-brown field on the horizon. Adam returned to the desk and opened Josef's work. It was ...

"Marvelous," he said aloud as he closed the last page a few hours later.

He stretched his arms above his head to relieve his stiffened back. He leaned into the upholstered leather armchair. A suggestion of a smile began forming in his eyes. He surrendered readily and allowed it to take over his entire face.

Adam Brandt knew exactly what he was going to do next.